I0777093

THE DEADLANDS
SPRING 2025

THE DEADLANDS

ISSUE 38, SPRING 2025

© 2025 by Psychopomp. All Rights Reserved.

ISBN-13: 979-8-89116-014-9

psychopomp.com

Publisher: Sean Markey
Editor in Chief: E. Catherine Tobler
Poetry Editor: Nicasio Andres Reed
Social Media: Felicia Martínez
Art Director: inkshark
Nonfiction Editor: David Gilmore
Necromancer at Large: Amanda Downum
Copy Editor: Laura Blackwell
Copy Editor: Annika Barranti Klein
Designer: Christine M. Scott
Cover: *A Furious Wind (The Plight of the Passenger Pigeon)* by Jenn Joslin

The Deadlands is distributed quarterly by:
 Psychopomp
 PO Box 36
 Woodbury, VT 05681

Subscriptions can be purchased at weightlessbooks.com. Individual issues can be obtained by joining our Patreon (with many deadly perks).
Join here: thedeadlands.com/patreon

SPRING 2025

TABLE OF CONTENTS

Poetry

TREATISE OF THE LYRIC ON THE STATE OF THINGS

Justin Cruzana

I.

After gutting and sublimating your victim into intent, you, hands the black of jeepney smoke, jar his remains. You tour him your turf of Manila, the streets of makeshift houses you once knew jollibee'd and private equity. Sunlight fills his glass like solace. Because what you offer is more than what the recipe requests of you, you prematurely daydream of days spent lounging in your high-rise soon-to-be loft, coffee you grabfood overpriced and beading with ice water the table. But in the house you look sideways thrice before entering (to make sure no one is there to turn you literary), you plug open the tv. War-torn countries as casual as poverty, yet has there been anything more lucrative than genocide. You flip back and forth the channels until the forecast corrects itself.

II.

Confessing to him my guilty pleasure of redirecting people through metaphor, my priest says along with three Hail Marys I must pay with my body. I say name your price. He says you must stave off from your fridge anything citrus, consume your caffeine with anything but black. Fasting so outdated our soon-to-be-canonized saints spend weeks in Makati, as punishment must down their shots with unmoder-ated restraint. Wanting my legacy to be as eternal as martyred red fighters, I tell my link hit me with the strongest you got. He whatsapps me headlines from the new york times. I shudder into the literal.

I.

The cross no longer symbol for anything. From a primer on past lives you tell your buddy I was what the car wanted with pleasure to eternalize. From absurdist to poet to director, the distinction moot. After lancing your newest victim (a man again, if it matters), his guts resin the september forever on your hands. Today you wash yourself of him by the birdbath so shrikes can reprise his sorrows tomorrow. A honda civic footnotes his misery from the city.

II.

The man I promise to meet has fewer emojis than I remember. If I tell him I spend most days knee-deep in phenomenology, will he ask me on a scale of one to truly how embarrassing is it to have a body. Because the postmodern is citational I give him page xvii, a coffee-stained page forty-four, a tweet from an account who with consistency posts decomposing collateral is hours away from suspension. He asks permission to give me what I (think I) want, his conviction as underdeveloped as sulphur. Tear away from my face empathy. State the position you want apartheid in this.

I.

You meet him through letterboxd to prove you are wont to kill someone without knowing his body. The fortitude of critics: you promise to sauté your next meal with a piece of his brain, maybe then the reconsideration with paris, texas. It was his knees you broke but seeing him see you with his torn-out twenty-twenty eyes you disbelieve any theory on the abled body. Distraught, you watch porn with no sound. Must it be his voice that rises from the muted man's mouth.

II.

O sword catcher, o death squad of lost souls, surely by impeding from me my destiny to ignite my free will you were fattening me up for glory all along. I face you on the sidewalks of death (Ermita)! Someone offers me another night and like the sinner turned saint I roll my tempted body down the hill. The breaking of waves captures me! I am what the seagulls stand on to sing to you, I am every zipper ripped open before pleasure, I am surf. While the conflict breaks me, I know elsewhere the fighting is real. Tell me how soon your arrival; will your presence somewhere else be the hurricane I must endure. Tell me how much / poetry I must skim through / until my name / begins to demand / his certainty

I.

You instagram story (but close friends only) the results. How sweet the real. While running to make true what already is, a beggar approaches you. He asks you for anything but the present tense. You piece up a cinnabar and put it on his hands. Above you, the oracled rain of heavenly fire. Loyal to its agenda, its embers turn your country into flowers.

HIGHWAY 1, PAST HOPE

Maria Haskins

LAYLA RISES like a breath in winter from the hollow beneath the black cottonwoods beside the river, shrugging off the blanket of dirt and leaves and centipedes she slept beneath. She should dissipate. She should waver and dissolve. She should ascend and alight. Instead, she starts gathering her bones.

Most of them are still in the hollow where he put her (clavicle, scapula, sternum). Some are scattered nearby, gnawed and cracked by teeth, beaks, claws (femur, tibia, humerus). A few are missing (rib, coccyx, metacarpals). The river has risen and receded many times since he left her here, its waters riffling through sediment and gravel, washing parts of her downstream, carrying them through the Fraser Canyon, underneath the bridges, past Surrey, New Westminster, and Richmond, maybe as far as the ocean. That's all right. What matters is that she's awake.

While Layla slept, dreams crawled and burrowed through her slumber, same as the worms and maggots burrowed through her flesh. Mostly, she dreamt about him. The smell of stale beer and pine air-freshener in his car. The smell of cigarettes and sweat. The taste of blood in her mouth. The way he held her. The way he held her down.

Layla knows only one thing could have stirred her from her sleep: he's back, and he is close.

She fits her bones together as best she can. And if some of the bones aren't exactly hers, if some of them are crow remnants, if there's an old bear skull beneath an alder she can use instead of her own shattered cranium, if there's a dog's sacral vertebra to replace what the coyotes took, no one's going to say anything about that. After all, the world is full of bones, forgotten, left behind, free for the taking.

By the time Layla is able to walk, the sun has almost gone down. Rocks and gravel crunch beneath her tarsals as she stalks away from the river. Crows caw as she passes, and a part of her, the part that's made of crow bones, wants to join them, longing for the warmth of feathers and company, the ritual of preening and roosting, but Layla has no time for the social niceties of birds.

She waves, and her finger bones rustle, feather-like, but she keeps going.

———

Penni's car runs out of gas westbound on Highway 1 just past Hope. She's been driving half a day from Kamloops after visiting her kids at her parents' place, and now it's evening and November and already dark at 5:00 p.m., the leaden clouds heavy with rain that isn't falling, yet. She feels like an idiot. The gas gauge is right there and probably the clunky old Ford's warning light has been shining for a while, but she took no notice and now she's here, pulled over on the shoulder with the Fraser River and the railroad tracks to her right, the mountains to her left, and home two hours ahead.

Joey's been texting her since Friday, asking why the fuck she left when he told her not to go, asking when she'll be back, and she hasn't replied because she doesn't want to get into it with him on the phone, but after a weekend of looking at her kids and pretending not to argue with her parents, she's too tired to deal with this shit. She texts Joey back and says that maybe she should get out and walk to a gas station or something. Hope isn't too far away after all. Or maybe she'll call a tow truck though she really can't afford it this month, what with the trip and all, or maybe she should just hitchhike the rest of the way to Surrey. Sure as shit she can't wait for the cops to pull over and try to help, not with an expired license and no insurance on the car. Joey texts back and asks her where she is, tells her to stay put, says he'll come get her. "Sit tight," he says.

He doesn't type "you dumb bitch," but it's there, spelled out between the lines.

Penni knows she should stay in the car and wait for him, but she doesn't. She gets out in the weeds by the roadside, cold hands deep in her jacket pockets, shoulders drawn up against the wind. Highway 1 is dark and mostly empty, just a few stray cars and semis roaring by, headed for Vancouver and the suburbs, or eastbound for the Coquihalla and the interior. The air is cold and smells like frost, her breath wavering in the dark. There's a smell in that cold air, beneath the frost, like dirt and wet leaves, like something rough and musty, dead or dying, threaded into the gathering darkness beneath.

A semitruck passes by so close it almost knocks Penni over, but after that the night goes silent, as if the rest of the world has receded and left her all alone. In that silence she hears the rustle of small lives moving through the blackberry brambles, hears the river whispering.

Her phone buzzes in her pocket. Maybe it's her parents or the kids, checking if she got home okay. Maybe it's Joey. She doesn't care anymore. It's too much, all of it. Them, her, him. Everything is too heavy to carry. The weight of her parents, of leaving her kids with them. The weight of knowing they've always been better off without her. The weight of Joey coming to get her, of knowing that she'll go home with him, again, no matter how foul his mood is by the time he gets here. It would be so much easier, wouldn't it, to shed all that weight, to go down to the river, and let the water carry her.

Penni opens the car door and puts her phone on the passenger seat. She takes a step into the bracken. The road is already far away.

———

Layla finds the new girl he brought to the river beneath a thin spread of leaves a ways downstream from the black cottonwoods. He isn't there. She was too slow, gathering her bones, and he's already been and gone, already did what he came here for. The girl's makeup is smudged, just like Layla's was the last time she had a face, and what's left of the girl's warmth is seeping into gravel and dirt. One part of Layla, the part of her that's a dog's vertebra, wants to stay and sniff the girl's hair and clothes, wants to nudge her with nose and paws, but Layla has no time for the rituals of dogs, no time to linger. Besides, what good would it do? Whenever this girl wakes, she'll have to gather her bones and find her own way out of here.

Layla isn't fast anymore, not like she used to be back when she could run faster than anyone else at school, but she increases her pace, striding up the steep slope to the wilting grass and flowers beside the roadway. Once she reaches the highway, the smell of asphalt and diesel and roadkill bring back more memories. She remembers a bar, her body steaming with sweat on the cramped dance floor, the music playing loud. That song she liked. The one she liked to dance to with her best friend. Arms in the air, eyes closed, the bass and drums a heartbeat, keeping her alive while they sang along, together. Too loud, off-key, perfect.

Layla remembers the rasp and rattle of her last breath. She remembers the way he put his hands on her. The way he put himself inside her.

A drift of rain slides down the mountainside as Layla lopes along the highway and in the glow from the passing headlights, she glistens. She whispers as she goes, her voice nothing like it used to be, her brassy girl's voice turned into the grinding, dry sound of wind through bones and teeth. She whispers the last words she remembers hearing and speaking: *don't hurt me leave me alone, fuck you fuck you fuck you no no no.*

It's a rough go for Penni, getting to the river. Beneath the dense underbrush the slope from the highway gives too easily beneath her runners, and there are rocks and pits and chunks of garbage hidden beneath the dead leaves and grass. Penni falls and scratches up her hands and knees. Her pants and shoes are soaked through by the time she crosses the train tracks and reaches the water.

In the deepening night, the river keeps its own light, a faint and shivering reflection of the cloudy night sky mirrored and rippling in dark water, ever moving, ever whispering. Penni crouches, dips her hand in the stream. It's cold. Colder than the darkness. Stronger too. Perhaps strong enough to carry her. She's been crying all day, ever since she left her parents' house, but she isn't crying anymore. The water moves past on its way to the coast and the ocean and all the other worlds beyond, places she has never seen and can never reach, and she just wants to find out what it's like to float for a while. To shed everything. To weigh nothing at all.

She doesn't see the man until she steps into the water.

He is standing at the river's edge downstream, a looming silhouette without face or features. She watches as he crouches, sits down on his haunches, hands moving in the water as if he's washing them, rinsing them clean in the current. In the dark, it's hard to gauge how far away he is, but Penni is close enough to hear him breathe. She can smell him too, and it's an all-too-familiar scent. Old sweat and stale beer. Cigarettes and booze.

Blood.

Penni doesn't know why she does what she does next. Maybe it's the shock of his presence, or maybe it's because she's just a fucking mess, but she blurts out a name, says it out loud, says, *Joey?*, even though she knows it can't be him. Her voice sounds brittle in the darkness, and the river's murmur is almost strong enough to cover it. Almost.

Even before the man turns, Penni knows she ought to run, knows it's too late, too, that there's nowhere to go except into the water or into the darkness. A dead end, either way.

———

Layla finds his SUV parked near a creek that hurries down the mountainside, passing underneath the highway through a cylinder of corrugated metal. It's the same car as when he drove her to the cottonwoods, but with a new pine air-freshener dangling from the rearview mirror.

He isn't there, but Layla knows he's close. She could wait for him here, by the road, or inside his car if she wanted to, but every part of Layla—girl, bear, crow, dog—is impatient, every bone she gathered is cracking with intent and purpose as she follows his trail along the creek, into the shadows, toward the river.

When the man turns toward Penni, he seems to grow larger, his shadowy shape bleeding into the night. Backing away, Penni feels the shallow current move around her ankles, her shoes sinking deeper into the loose sediment and smooth pebbles the river has gathered at its edges. The man straightens his back as he turns, as he sees her. Maybe he says something. Maybe she says, "my boyfriend's coming to get me," a useless incantation at the best of times, but especially in a place like this. Maybe he takes a step closer. Maybe he's coming for her, fast and heavy. Maybe there's something in his hand now, metal, edge, sharp, maybe it's a knife, maybe it was a knife he was cleaning in the water, or maybe it's all just shadows and water, maybe the entire world is a hollow space to hold the shape of him, the shape of her, in the darkness, forever. Penni isn't sure what she sees and then she sees nothing at all because something strong and fast knocks her off her feet from behind. She lands hard, flat on her back in the water, nothing to break her fall except spine and skull, and there is a shape in the water, rushing past her, a bear or dog, maybe, or something else her brain can't make sense of. There's a scream that might be hers or might be someone else's and then she's gone, under water, under the rocks, under the surface of the world.

When Layla first awoke, she couldn't name the feeling that stirred her from her sleep. It was like the tip of a knife, like steel jiggling through skin and flesh, ever closer to the marrow, the warmth of it gushing gushing gushing like blood, if she'd still had flesh to pierce and blood to spill.

Layla knows the name of the feeling that overcomes her when she finds him by the river, and the name of that feeling is *joy.*

The last time they were together, she didn't understand what he wanted. Now, she knows. Now, she can show him all the things he showed her, can do all the things he likes to do. Tearing down the slope, knocking aside branches and shadows, splashing through the water, she doesn't stop until she's close enough to touch him. For the glimmer of a second, she stops and pulls herself together, her bones rattling and clacking, rustling and chittering as she rises to her full height, facing him.

That part of Layla that is a bear's skull, with a bear's teeth and jaws, roars. It roars the words he said to her back at him, all the words Layla dreamt of since he left her beneath the cottonwoods. *Shut up shut up shut your fucking face I'll kill you I'll fucking kill you. Bitch do you like it bitch.* And then she does what she has been longing for, dreaming of, she does to him what he did to her, all those things he likes, all those things he wants, she puts herself inside him, the way he likes to do, her bones and teeth cutting through him, into him, ripping him open. She puts herself inside him, pushing herself into the holes and hollows of his body, and the skull of a bear that is Layla's skull now, keeps roaring the words he said, the words he hissed into her ear as she bled out, and she knows he loves it because he screams and screams as she puts her hands on him, as she puts her hands inside him, dislodging his bones and organs, taking him apart, and he must like it, but then he stops screaming and now he's quiet and now he's gone.

The river takes what's left of him and washes Layla clean. It washes away the pieces clinging to her phalanges and metacarpals, to her mandible and manubrium. The river flows into her and through her and keeps on going to the ocean. That's all right. She's still here.

Layla is still half-submerged in the river's whirlpools and eddies when she sees the woman in the water. She is face-down, sinking, brown hair floating in the current. Layla grabs hold of her, turns her over in the water, and all the parts of Layla that was a girl, all those parts of her that liked to sing too loud, off-key, with a best friend who couldn't help her in the end, all those parts of Layla know exactly what to do.

Penni wakes near the top of the slope by the highway, her soaking-wet jacket and jeans tangled in blackberry brambles. She is freezing cold, teeth chattering, her throat and chest aching like she's been puking her guts out, and her head hurts like a motherfucker. Probing her skull with numb fingers she finds a lump behind her ear, maybe a cut or fracture, and it wouldn't be the first time someone cracked her skull, but at least she can move, at least she can stand.

Her eyes aren't working properly, her vision's muddled from river water or tears or maybe from passing out. The man she saw by the river is gone, and whatever knocked her down is gone too. Somehow she got herself out of the water, across the train tracks, and up the slope. She doesn't know how. It's all a muddle of cold and darkness, but the car is where she left it, pulled over on the shoulder, and behind it, lit up from inside, Joey's car.

Even though her vision is still gauzy, she sees Joey throw his car door open and stride toward her. She knows that gait, that swing of the arms, that tilt of his head, knows what it means, knows what's coming even before he grabs her arm and smacks her in the face. Open hand, not the fist at least. The pain of it, layered on top of all the other pain in her body, barely registers, but she stumbles to her knees before he hauls her up and drags her to his car.

She isn't sure if he hits her again before she gets into her seat, and she might have tried to tell him what happened, might have asked him if he saw the man with the knife or maybe he didn't have a knife at all, and maybe there was a dog or a bear, but there is no space for her words right now because Joey is shouting at her, all the usual things he says when he's disappointed in her.

As they drive away, leaving her car stranded on the roadside because Joey doesn't have time for this fucking bullshit right now, Penni puts her hand in her pocket, looking for her phone. It isn't there because it's where she left it, on the seat of her car, maybe still buzzing, the kids wondering where she is, if she made it home, but what would she say if she could answer? What would she tell them this time? Penni thinks about them, on the porch, watching her drive away. She didn't want to leave them. She didn't want to come back here. Why did she?

The phone isn't there, but tucked into the pocket's lining Penni finds something else. A small, uneven object. To her fingers, it feels at first like a pebble from the river, but when she looks at it in the glow from the dashboard, as her fingers travel over its ridges and divots, she realizes it's a small piece of bone.

Penni closes her eyes and lets her fingers worry at the bone while Joey keeps shouting at her. There's a smell in the car, or maybe the smell is coming from her, a smell of leaves and dirt and water, and she might have said something about it, but Joey isn't listening and maybe it doesn't matter. She tastes blood in her mouth, feels the bruises coming where he grabbed her, and something stirs inside her, then, a feeling she can't name, not yet. But it's there, like the tip of a knife, like steel jiggling through skin and flesh, gushing gushing gushing like blood.

It's the dog part of Layla, that single sacral vertebra, that makes her get into the car while the man is busy shouting. The dog remembers car rides and sticking his head out the window and Layla, well, she doesn't mind a car ride, not anymore. The crow and bear parts of her would rather have stayed by the river, beneath the trees, but they can wait. Layla can always find her way back to the canyon, to the river, to the black cottonwoods.

She could dissipate. She could waver and dissolve. She could ascend and alight. Instead, her bones are tucked in neatly on the floor behind the passenger seat while the man drives down the highway. Layla likes to listen to him. She wants to know the kinds of things he likes to say, the kinds of things he likes to do. She wants to know everything about him.

Gathering herself together on the car floor, Layla flexes her right hand, bones rustling quietly like wings, like crows coming home to roost. There's a missing distal phalanx on that hand, but that's all right. The world is full of bones, forgotten, left behind, free for the taking. Enough for Layla. Enough for anyone else who might stir in her wake.

Fiction

SOUL SHEPHERDS

Joshua Lim

ACROSS the ruined fields came the faint boom of artillery shells in the distance. Standing silently among the blackened grasses, the Grim Reaper leaned on his scythe and waited, his black robes billowing around his tall frame in the cold northern breeze. The smell of noxious fumes and death filled the air. There were souls to collect, but the Reaper had something more important to deal with first.

Angels began to descend from the heavens. They glided down through the clouds or came drifting across the plains from nearby cities, summoned by the news of the crash. Most of them were white-robed angels from European countries, but there were also several Arabic malaikats and various soul shepherds from other beliefs among them—crows, owls, a couple of wrinkled ancestor spirits, and a regal god from the Indian subcontinent. A few nodded in greeting to the Grim Reaper as they passed by.

The Reaper paid them no mind. He was waiting only for Kondok.

The smoky evening air shimmered, the grassy ground split open to reveal a portal from the underworld. A strong, brown-skinned young man leapt into the world of the living. He wore nothing but a traditional Mah Meri skirt of woven pandanus leaves around his waist.

This was Moyang Kondok, the soul shepherd from Malaysia. His haunted expression showed that news of the tragedy had struck him hard.

"You came alone," said the Reaper.

"We are shorthanded at home, in case you haven't been paying attention."

That terse response was uncharacteristic of Kondok. Among spirits, no one dared speak so bluntly to the Grim Reaper. Yet everyone knew that in stressful times even soul shepherds could lose their professionalism, so a few rough words could be excused.

"Patience, Moyang Kondok." The Reaper's voice was a quiet hiss between his teeth. "Do not act in anger. Remember your vows."

Kondok ignored him and strode past him towards the crash site. The Reaper glided after him and laid a skeletal hand on his shoulder. Kondok knocked it off, but the Reaper caught him again and held firmly this time, his fingerbones digging into the moyang's bare skin.

"Out of my way, Reaper," growled Kondok.

"Not until you calm down."

"I have work to do!"

"You are not fit to shepherd souls in this mood," the Reaper said firmly. "Let us handle everything for you, just this time."

"You have your people to guide, and I have mine. They await me!"

Kondok tore free from the Reaper's grasp and stormed towards the plane's wreckage. The Reaper exhaled strongly through his skull and followed closely behind.

The growing darkness on the Ukrainian plains forced all first responders to switch on their searchlights in order to continue their harrowing work. While angels and humans wandered among the fallen debris, Kondok stopped at the edge of the ruin and stood gazing at a world thick with sorrow and death.

At his feet lay a suitcase, open. Clothes spilled out; some large, some small. Beside them lay a wallet among scattered personal belongings.

Kondok picked up the wallet and flipped it open. The vibrant faces of a young woman and her infant smiled back at him from the clear window in the front pocket. Gently he replaced the wallet where it had fallen.

Around him, firefighters scoured the unsalvageable wreckage of the passenger plane. Journalists hovered at the distant edges of the wreck, snapping photos and taking notes, the weight of the tragic loss of life evident upon their pale and haggard faces. They were surrounded and monitored by armed rebels from the battalion that had shot down the plane. Beyond the smoking fuselage lay what remained of the wings, cabin, landing gear and fuel tanks, no more than heaps of crumpled metal. Everywhere Kondok looked, there were pieces of debris, luggage, and bodies—unnumbered bodies, strewn everywhere.

The tail of the plane lay alone in a separate field, sticking out of the soil. Kondok drew near and stood beneath the shadow of the twisted steel, staring silently at the red-and-blue logo printed on it, clenching and unclenching his fists.

The Grim Reaper hung back, watching Kondok carefully. He had to make sure that the moyang did not lose control of himself. The other soul shepherds had discussed their concerns and had unanimously elected the Reaper to keep an eye on him, but now the Reaper was starting to doubt whether he could control Kondok if anything went wrong.

Thankfully, backup arrived.

"Moyang Kondok," someone called.

Kondok and the Reaper turned.

Two ghostly figures approached them, wreathed in wispy clouds formed by their powerful aura, their feet touching the ground so lightly that they glided more than walked. Kondok knew this duo; he had met them in Malaysia many times when receiving souls from Chinese funerals. They were recognizable from their matching robes and tall hats, the chains and hand fans that they carried, and their contrasting colour schemes: the taller one clad entirely in white, the other in black.

They were the Heibai Wuchang—the Ghosts of Impermanence, the twin soul shepherds from Chinese folk beliefs.

"Greetings, Reaper. Greetings, Kondok," said the slender and elegant White Guard with a gentle smile. "It has been a long time since we last met. Last September, was it?"

"It was December," said Kondok, bowing in return. "Greetings to you too, First and Second Masters." That was the proper way to address the Heibai Wuchang. Soul shepherds who worked in the same region were often more courteous to their colleagues. As he bowed, he missed the glance of understanding between the Grim Reaper and the Heibai Wuchang.

"Shall we proceed in our duties?" said the short and swarthy Black Guard.

"Yes we shall," said the Reaper.

They joined the other soul shepherds in the acknowledgement of the dead.

Angels walked through the plain of death, their wings folded, laying their gentle hands on every broken body they could find. Many angels were weeping, golden tears streaming down their faces and splashing onto the silent forms. It mattered not what religious beliefs the deceased had held in life. For soul shepherds, every death deserved to be mourned. They spoke not a word as they anointed each body they found.

Kondok was no fool. It did not take long for him to notice that the Heibai Wuchang and the Reaper did not leave his side as they walked together through the field of debris. Finally, exasperated, he swung around to face them.

"Stop following me. Don't you have your own souls to seek?"

"Kondok, we are here for your sake," said the White Guard.

"I do not need your constant supervision!" snapped Kondok. "I have been a soul shepherd for a thousand years. I can do my duty without you looking over my shoulder, thank you very much!"

"This isn't about your work." The Reaper's eyes glowed in their empty holes. "We cannot allow you to attack the humans who have caused this tragedy. That would destroy the peace, and it would be disastrous for everyone."

"You are angry," the Black Guard added. "We understand. But valid or not, you are in danger of breaking your vows if you lash out."

"Vows?" Kondok half-laughed, half-cried. "Our vows of neutrality? Vows of standing aside, vows of doing nothing while our wards perish. Do you know who were the neutral ones here, Reaper?" He jabbed his finger at the ghastly scenes surrounding them. "All these people were neutral. Every single one of them, and now they are dead!"

Before they could speak, Kondok leapt into the air with a burst of power and sped towards the armed men who were policing the first responders.

"Kondok, stop!"

Kondok flew through the air, fists raised, radiating power, ready to smash the puny humans into pulp. The mortals would never stand a chance. They deserved every conceivable punishment in hell for the terror they had unleashed upon the passengers in the plane.

Avenge those poor souls, ran the burning thoughts through Kondok's mind, passion coursing through his veins, his senses blinded by fury. *Give these killers what they deserve, they have slain hundreds of innocents, send them straight to hell, avenge the dead, avenge them…*

Another few seconds and it would have been too late.

The Black Guard's long chain wrapped around Kondok's feet and dragged him back to earth. The White Guard's hand fan blew a strong gust of wind that knocked the Malaysian spirit over backwards. Kondok gasped, trying to catch his breath. The Grim Reaper placed his heavy, bony foot on the moyang's chest and pressed him to the ground.

"This is your final warning, Kondok," said the Reaper in a stern voice laced with authority. The curved blade of his scythe glinted. "If you try anything again, on my word as a senior shepherd, you shall be stripped of your powers and blacklisted forever."

A few nearby angels approached warily with their swords drawn, ready to lend a hand if necessary. The Heibai Wuchang Guards waved them away, assuring them that the Reaper was in control. Peace between deities of various cultures was maintained in part by the cooperation between soul shepherds, and most spirits would not hesitate to help others uphold the law in dire situations.

Tears pooled in Kondok's eyes, and he began to weep.

"It's not fair," he managed to say. "They didn't deserve this."

Does anyone deserve anything? the Reaper wanted to respond. As soul shepherds, it was not in their place to judge. There were greater spirits in the various underworlds and afterlives who would take care of that. Soul shepherds were only there to mourn, comfort and guide. All spirits who took on the role were made to understand this.

But the Reaper said nothing, for he understood that Kondok needed to vent and struggle through all the tumultuous emotions he was facing.

"May the innocent be avenged and the guilty be damned," said the White and Black Guards in unison. That was their declaration every time they guided souls.

The fire faded from Kondok's eyes. For a brief moment his veneer of glamour fell apart, and his true appearance came through: a tired face worn by years of unnumbered tears that had etched faint grey tracks down his cheeks, his deep black eyes lined with immeasurable sadness. For a fraction of a second, the deaths and lives of millions of souls, young and old, were reflected in the dark pupils of he who had been their final companion before they entered the afterlife.

Then he brushed away his tears, and he became a young man lying on the grass again.

"May I get up?" Kondok asked.

"First recite your vows again," the Grim Reaper said. "To remind yourself of the great task we undertake."

In their presence Kondok uttered the solemn words.

"I am a shepherd of souls. My ears are closed to mortal quarrels; I stand apart from all sides. My eyes are closed to judgement; I see neither sinner nor saint. My hands consecrate the fallen, my feet tread the shadowed paths where none should walk alone. I am the guardian of the last journey, the final companion, the eternal and impartial guide."

The last light of the sun, no more than a streak of yellow on the horizon, sank and vanished at last. The fields of wheat and debris were plunged into the gloom of night—and slowly, among the angels, translucent beings begin to take form. Some wandered aimless; others sat beside their bodies, quiet. A few were trying to wake themselves up. Under the light of the stars, they begin to glimmer as the last vestiges of physicality seeped out from their spiritual forms.

Human souls.

"Our wards are here," said the Reaper. Without saying farewell he took his foot off Kondok's chest and turned away, his black robes swishing softly.

The Guards helped Kondok to his feet and brushed the grass off his body.

"Let us do our duty without delay and leave this place," said the Black Guard, and the others agreed.

The main passenger cabin, mangled and crushed, was where most of the angels and spirits gathered. In most deaths, the human souls could be found sitting beside their deceased earthly shells, but in accidents like these where everything in the aircraft had been scattered over leagues of land, sometimes it took days to find the souls who had been separated from their bodies.

As Kondok and the Heibai Wuchang approached, a tall angel with a scroll hailed them. He did not seem to recognize them. That was expected, as Asian soul shepherds rarely visited this corner of the world.

"You're the Chinese psychopomps, I presume?" The angel gestured at their matching black-and-white attire. "Heibai Wuchang, the White and Black Guards?"

"That is us."

The angel placed a hand on his heart—a sign of empathic respect and mourning between soul shepherds. "We mourn with you." He ran a finger down his scroll. "You have two souls to escort today. An old woman and a middle-aged man. May your journey be smooth."

The Guards nodded and moved towards the wreckage.

The angel frowned at Kondok. "I don't recognise you. Where are you from?"

"I am a soul shepherd from Malaysia. My name is Moyang Kondok, the Spirit of the Pangolin from the Mah Meri pantheon."

"Malaysia? Where are Tok Samin and Che Timah?"

"They sent me in their stead," Kondok said. "They are busy… They've been working in the Indian Ocean for the past four months."

The angel's expression changed. "I am sorry." He placed his hand on his heart again. "It has been a hard year for your country. We mourn with you."

The Heibai Wuchang emerged from the cabin, guiding two glowing souls. The White Guard gave Kondok a final bow of farewell, then the spirits sank into the ground with their wards and disappeared into the Chinese underworld. A small white lily blossom sprouted at the spot where they vanished.

"You have one soul waiting for you over there," said the angel, pointing towards the nearby woods. As Kondok was leaving, the angel continued, "I didn't know that people still followed the old religions of the indigenous tribes. There were no Mah Meri names on the passenger list."

Kondok shook his head. "I'm not here because they believe in me. I do the same duty as the Grim Reaper." He pointed across the field.

The majority of souls had departed with the angels, leaving several stragglers sitting dumbfounded among the debris. Over them now loomed a giant hooded shape, blacker than the night sky, blotting out the bright stars. With his gleaming scythe resting on his shoulder, as he passed by each soul, the Reaper tapped them on their shoulders with a skeletal finger. The souls rose one by one and entered his embrace, disappearing into the folds of his robes.

"Those who do not adhere to a specific belief or another, the Grim Reaper takes under his wing," Kondok said with a sombre smile. "In Malaysia, they come under my care."

He entered the woods.

Under a smoking chunk of cabin that had been flung into the trees, the soul of a young woman sat, silent. Her body was nowhere to be seen, likely buried somewhere under the rubble. As Kondok walked up to her, she looked up.

Moyang Kondok saw her entire life through her eyes. Virtuous deeds, evil deeds, desires, struggles, loves and hates, victories and regrets. The urge to pronounce her saint or sinner rose in his heart as usual, but he pushed it aside. This was a human life in all its glory and shame—but it was not his place to judge.

He was merely a soul shepherd, after all.

Kondok extended his hand. "Come, my daughter."

She took his hand. Together they walked out of the quiet woods and down the long dark road where the booming echoes of artillery shells could reach them no more.

In memory of the victims of MH17 and MH370

WHALESONG

Guan Un

THE WHALESONG hits when she's on the highway.

Up until that point, Hailey had just been driving, foot tensed on the pedal, hoping velocity would turn into an answer for a question that she didn't know. There had been arguments, words at volume, a heat inside her that had incinerated most of what he had said apart from a few fragments: *too sensitive, always make such a big deal out of everything. And the biggest one: what do you actually want?*

Instead she has a car, a heart full of ash, and a feeling that approaches mourning every time she slows down.

So she speeds up. The Australian countryside slides past the windows, purple lantana clutching metal fences, chessboards of grapevines, patient hills—

—which is when the whalesong keens into her head.

It almost makes her crash when the song bursts upon her all at once—she doesn't know how she knows it's a whalesong but she does—as it keens and lists, sorrowful and sick, like a misshapen clarinet turned up in the speakers, the notes outstretched hands, flailing out to find *something.*

What do I do? Is this a stroke? Am I going crazy? She brakes hard, pulls into the slow lane, almost causes an accident. There's the scream of car horns as cars veer around her but she barely hears it over the whalesong.

Did I accidentally play some music? She glances at her phone in the dock but there's nothing playing, just a notification about the six missed calls.

She doesn't know what else to do so she dials him back.

"H—? Where are you?" His voice comes through the speakers but she can barely hear it over the whalesong.

"I just…can you hear that?" Hailey asks. Her voice seems faraway.

"What are you being s— about now?"

"You can't hear it?"

"Stop m— things up. Just come b— and we c— …"

That's when she sees the sign, white letters on green: Historic Whaling Station—Next Turnoff. The whalesong ascends an octave and then doubles back on itself.

She has a choice. She could turn around. She could go back.

Instead she ends the call and takes the turnoff. The road enters a national park and winds down into a valley. She slows into the turns. Eucalyptus trees pile high into the sky, the decadent tumble of the greenery—it would be beautiful if she wasn't doubting her own head. Her fingers tighten on the peeling steering wheel. The song takes on a different texture; the whalesong arcs up then moans back down, a distorted trombone sliding down the register.

As she pulls into the parking lot, she finds a tear running down her face and something pulling at her gut like reverse hunger. She rubs the tear away with a sleeve, slams the door of her car.

She is suddenly aware of how adrift she is, only a whalesong to guide her. She doesn't even know what she's looking for, what she would do if she found whatever it was.

To distract herself, she surveys the whaling station. Just a few wood buildings, splitting the difference between historic and run-down. Beyond those, the enticing waterline in turquoise bleeding into the blue, and a gravel path that leads down to a long stone slipway that edges onto the shore, a platform the size of a parking lot, and Hailey knows, or maybe the song tells her: this is where they did the killing.

The song pulls her down the steps, past the sign that advertises "Tours at 10 a.m. and 2 p.m.!," past another sign that tells her this is the Flensing Deck, where a solid woman in a Parks uniform waves to her from the edge of the platform.

"H—!" the ranger says, but it's impossible to hear much over the whalesong. Hailey does her best to focus on the ranger's lips. "Are you h— for the t—?"

Hailey is trying to frame a response when the corpse behind the ranger comes into focus. There are chains bisecting half of the deck and a Restricted Area sign, and beyond that there is the body of a whale, the mass of it filling the edge of the flensing deck. Blood gouts from the wound on its belly, dark red, almost black and almost beautiful. One of its eyes rotates to peer at Hailey and it keens, and *keens* so that Hailey finds herself covering her ears and shrinking from the sound.

"You o—? Hon?" asks the ranger.

"I'm…" *Not okay,* Hailey thinks. "I'm fine. A little dizzy," is what she manages to say. It's an effort not to shout the words.

It's not real, of course. If a giant whale carcass was actually on the platform, then the ranger wouldn't be standing here exchanging platitudes. If a giant whale carcass was there, she'd be able to smell it. But it's difficult to argue with the song, the pleading voice that is spilling through her head.

"Just d—, huh?" says the ranger with something in her eyes like suspicion. To be fair, Hailey knows she must look a little unhinged, but she is struggling to care.

She forces herself to stand, bring her arms down by her sides. And she forces herself to look, to really look at the whale corpse, and she sees the way it shimmers at the edges like a tarmac under heat. *A ghost?* She isn't sure if that is better or worse.

Hailey walks around closer to the chains when the ranger's voice stops her. "S—hon, gotta k— b-hind the chains."

"Can I just—" Hailey begins.

The ranger gives her a strange look. "I'm s—, ma'am, we don't want any d—mage, historical site and all."

Boundaries. But I'm great at boundaries, Hailey says to herself. The thought almost sends her into another giggle fit.

The whale's eye wanders around to meet Hailey's. *I'm coming,* she thinks. And maybe the song gets lower, or maybe she's getting used to the chaos in her head.

"Uh, the tour," Hailey says. "When's the tour?"

The ranger checks her wristwatch. "2 p.m. Oh, I better get r—. Meet me b— at the car p— in five."

Hailey nods, waits until the ranger is out of sight, then ducks under the chains.

It's so big up close. She could curl up inside the whale's stomach, she thinks, and it would barely notice.

She reaches a hand slowly towards its skin and her hand passes through it. It's translucent. A hallucination then. But at least it was a beautiful one, even in dying, the slow, soft curves of it, the way its muscles ripple under thick skin.

"Now what do I do with you?" Hailey asks, half to herself. The whale watches her, waiting for her to understand, and Hailey feels tears falling from her.

"I'm sorry," she says, "that someone did this to you."

Her gut pulls at her again and there's a blue thread running down from the whale's body to her own. A ghostly umbilical cord. This she can touch. And as she pulls it experimentally, the whale's body moves too. The song increases, with a counterpoint of joy.

"But where?" Hailey asks.

And the whale's eye turns around, to the only answer that was possible—the blue welcome of the water.

Hailey begins to pull. The strangest thing is that it's heavy. Not as heavy as its physical body, of course, but Hailey sweats as she pulls the whale's body down the ramp, towards the water. One step, then another, easing the whale down to the waves.

And then she hears voices.

The tour.

"And here," the ranger's voice, "is the flensing deck, where they did the damage." The ranger leads two adults and two kids with permanent eyerolls onto the top half of the deck.

Hailey freezes for a moment. She's not even sure what she could say. "I was just cleaning up this ghost whale for you"? But her eyes meet the ranger's. Then the ranger's eyes slide down to the thread in Hailey's hands and across to the body of the whale. An understanding passes between them: a common vocabulary of pain. The ranger nods.

"And down there is one of our volunteers, helping us to clean up," says the ranger. But the family's eyes pass over her, already bored.

Hailey takes another step back, shoes into the water, salt splashing on skin. As she pulls, she can feel the ache of it in her heart, in her stomach. Then the angle of the thread moves upwards, the whale rising above the ground, its tail beginning to kick.

The song changes, lessens in her head but then grows, not in volume but in voice, and as she looks up, she understands: the song has called and a chorus of whalesongs answer back. Up above her, thirty or forty whales swim through the air, all a-song, circling like a halo.

The ghost of the whale (she is so tempted to call it hers) is above the waves now and its liquid eyes fix on Hailey's.

"It's okay," Hailey says. "It's okay! You don't have to stay."

Hailey lets go and the thread detaches. The whale turns once more, its tail flipping in a salute, and it swims upwards through the sky to join the throng. A lightness shakes through every part of Hailey's body: the sensation of becoming free.

Poetry

AFTER THE STORM

Ishita Basu Mallik

When I go back, months later
to warm tired bones,
clipped-wing ducks preen in the shallows

Their feeding frenzy ripples out,
a scatter of water lilies swaying
in uncanny light

Geese bellow in the distance
but water hyacinth claims territory faster
in an uprising of fat green fists

The path between trees and water
swirls in a slant shimmer—
rumors of a portal in plain sight

Now that it already happened, there's a boat
quick response rescue
its two young crewmen awaiting worse

Leaving them behind, an eye opens
in quiet assessment— a dog's silent witness
and old trees weaving over wettest dark

A boat pierces the skin
of awareness. Oars swing and push
in solemn ritual of a forgotten creed

Eternity ends before the boat
scrolls offscreen
humid heat muffling Coach's shouts

A large fish rockets to surface, gasping
Water crosses water
like beaded curtains stirred by many hands

Farther, where it's stillest, cormorants crowd
a krishnochura branch.
Blue-eyed ferrymen of deepest depths,

There is much they have known—
air turned deadweight in hollow hulls
sudden storms' sorrows

Nonfiction

JOHN

Penelope K. Parker

I'VE NEVER BEEN a fan of the outdoors, but you already knew that. I've always squirmed with fear when a bee buzzed by, scurrying away at the sight of anything with a stinger. I refuse to sit on the grass without a towel to protect my clothes from dirt, and my body of water of choice is always indoors and chlorinated. It makes sense that I swore off hiking at a young age.

I never understood the appeal of intentionally submerging myself in the elements—with no escape from the crawling insects with too many legs to count, sludge-like mud that glues itself to the bottom of my shoes to leave a brown trail for weeks, and dirt that would get caught under my fingernails no matter how hard I tried to avoid it.

I wonder how surprised you would be, to see me now approaching the peak of Mount Lagazuoi, with my frizzy hair pulled back into a tight pony and decked out in barely broken-in hiking boots. Thinking of your reaction makes me smile.

"You? Hiking?" you would say, with a skeptical grin on your face. "What happened to the Penelope I know?"

And then we'd both laugh, and I'd tell you of all my adventures in the mountains of the Dolomites, Italy. I'd show you all the embarrassing photos my new friends took of me, sweaty and out of breath from the smallest of hills. I'd share the unique moments I witnessed with other hikers along the way, all more experienced than me: the Dutch couple with the poofy white dog, the two elderly women who stopped every two minutes to take a photo together, and the little girl who waved at me from her father's shoulders.

"You have to see the mountains yourself," I would say to you, knowing you can't.

I would go on about the carefully balanced cairns sprinkled across the sea of rocks, the crisp gusts of air that whipped my hair around into knots, the breathtaking view from the peak.

Can you believe that for the first time, I wasn't annoyed that my hair was a mess from the wind?

My bangs stood straight up, and I took pictures anyway. You wouldn't recognize me.

The Lagazuoi mountainside was littered with wildflowers. Small patches of blues, pinks, yellows, and whites contrasted with the green grass and beige rocks like splotches of acrylic paint on a wooden palette. The white marguerite daisies reminded me of you. They always have.

The white petals sprouted out from the chalky, yellow center. The emerald stems jumped up from patches of flat dirt and in between pebbles and stones. The daisies bobbed their heads with the wind, appearing in my line of view when I least expected. The perennial plant never vacates the mountainside—but the individual blossoms will wither quickly and bud again somewhere else. A symbol of a short, but beautiful, life. The bittersweet pang of a goodbye, and the promise of meeting again. I've learned to appreciate the bloom while it lasts.

I posed my arm right beside two blossoms, perfectly mirroring the inked petals permanently etched onto the skin of my forearm. I wanted to pluck one and bring it back to you— maybe I would hang it beside the old, dried roses I stole from your bed all those years ago—but I decided not to disturb the mountain.

"I'm no hiker," you would say. I know you're not. You've got a bad knee, from an accident long before I was alive. "I couldn't do all that, not like you can."

"But you did. Remember Hawaii?" I would ask, shaking my head.

You climbed to the top of the Diamond Head State Monument with Mom, around twenty years ago. I wasn't born yet, but I've seen the pictures.

The day was blazing hot, the sun was beating down and burned the top of your shoulders dark pink. You wore one of your signature Harley Davidson baseball caps to hide your frizz, and Mom wore her vintage denim shorts with a daisy patch on the left back pocket and a new pair of crisp white sneakers. She complained about those shoes the entire hike; they dug into her aching arches. Do you remember that day?

The stairs went up so high, they vanished into the sky before you could see the top. Mom was terrified of those steps. They were steep and daunting. The only assistance was two metal beams which served as a rusted railing. You smiled at her, with that reassuring twinkle in your green eyes that my mother and I never failed to find comfort in. She tells me I have your eyes.

You took her hand in your own. The stairway was tight, but you managed to squeeze her in by your side, remaining next to each other until you both reached the top. When you finally made it, the two-hour hike was suddenly made worth it, or so I'm told.

"The water was gorgeous," you would say to me.

The photograph you took proves that. The bright blue water can be seen crashing into the shore from a long distance away. Plots of green land with picnic blankets and kids playing baseball are surrounded by darker trees. The natural landscape slowly fades into a bustling, urban city. Bright green pastures shift into dreary blocks and squares of shiny grays, from left to right.

The ocean connects it all.

"I can see," I would say. "You were able to make it to the top that time."

"My knee killed me," you would say. I always forget about your bad knee. It gave you a limp, and then a cane.

"But you still made it. Why not try it again, one more time?" I would ask, with a glint of hope in my eyes—your eyes.

I imagine you hiking up Mount Lagazuoi with me. I would look upward at the steep incline made of rocks that have been worn down over the years, offering you a fearful expression that would remind you of Mom in Hawaii. You would take my hand with a gentle squeeze, just as you took hers. I recognize the reassuring twinkle in your eyes from the old photos. Side by side, we would slowly make our way to the summit. We would stop together by the pale log benches lining the pathway, resting and gazing across the Dolomites. You would share your observations and crack jokes with me about the little details you'd notice about other hikers.

"They're going to hate washing that dog later."

"Don't you think they've taken enough pictures?"

"I carried you like that when you were little."

We would be smiling and laughing so much, we'd hardly pay attention to the burning of our calves from the hike. Before we could realize it, we would reach the summit.

The summit of Mount Lagazuoi has a tall, wooden crucifix in memory of the lives lost there during World War I. It is displayed near the peak, one of the highest accessible points of Lagazuoi—this leads back to the early Christians, who believed the higher a place of worship, the closer one would be to the Heavens. A few wildflowers scattered across the ground nearby, with daisies and poppies that were sprinkled down from the sky above shyly peeking out from behind loose stones. The white and red blossoms mixed together on the mountain. The daisies purified the land, the poppies painted the blood that was spilled from the young men who were sent to their deaths up the same path we stand before. Solemnly gazing out at the scene, you would bow your head and say a quick prayer, as you would standing before any crucifix. With my head up, I only observe.

I slowly walked over to the journal beside the cross. I left you to have your moment by the crucifix. I'm sure you would believe we could reach Heaven from this point on the mountain. You were always more religious than me, anyways. You always believed there was an outside force at play. You often would tell me to have faith. I never did.

I opened the journal, immediately noticing the numerous signatures from countless dates and in countless languages. Pen in hand, I signed my name. And then I signed yours. I turned around to show you our signatures, which are separated. The paper, crowded with foreign letters and splotches of black and blue ink, caused our written names to reach far across the page, never quite touching one another.

But there is no one standing by the summit cross. There is nothing but a stray marguerite rooted firmly in the ground and delicately swaying in the wind. You aren't there. You never were.

"Penelope." Your distant voice calls me back to this limbo I've manifested.

"You know why."

I'm reminded of my question. I'm embarrassed I asked. Of course I know why you can't try hiking again. It's not because of your knee.

I don't like to think about it. I watched the familiar twinkle in your eyes fade over time. I remember when your frizzy hair was shaved and never grew back right. I couldn't count how many pill bottles lined your bedside table. I saw the limp gradually worsen until you needed a cane, and then a chair, and then a bed. A bedridden cancer patient cannot hike a mountain.

You will never experience the refreshingly cold air I inhaled at the peak of Mount Lagazuoi. Instead, you were confined to your stark white prison cell at the peak of a hill in a small New York town with church bells chiming multiple times a day. You found them comforting, just like the ornate crucifix hung above your bed. I found them incessant. The only fresh air you received was allowed in through a small crack in your one window, which offered you a perfectly framed view of a stone statue of the Virgin Mary overrun with moss and emerging out of a sea of budding daisies. Even with that window, your room reeked of rubbing alcohol and hospital linen. Years later, I don't know what, or who, your room reeks of anymore.

I've grown out of the clothes you last saw me in. My short, straight hair grew longer and developed the frizz you once had. I'm taller now, and I have changed. I wear the marguerite daisy in ink on my arm to honor your short, but beautiful, life. But I still haven't found the strength to visit your new bed, not since that dark December day that you were first laid in it. If I did, you wouldn't recognize me.

I think back to the Mount Lagazuoi summit. Staring out into the Italian landscape, I was convinced it couldn't be real. A bee buzzed by my head, and I flinched on the wooden log I perched myself upon. The little girl and her father walk past me once again. I watch her toddle over to a patch of white marguerites, pluck one with sticky fingers and offer it up to her dad. I regret not doing the same, until I remember the two signatures I left in the summit journal, and smile. You may be gone, but your name will be read.

THE TWELVE DEATHS OF YOU

C. J. Subko

CW: self-harm, birth, dead child, child sexual assault, abortion, murder, sex

AN OPEN GRAVE *is Mother Earth's cunt.* That's what he tells you, just before he teaches you how to dig your first grave. You are knives and needles as you stand on a patch of loamy earth under the baking sun, holding a sturdy metal shovel.

Eight feet by two-and-a-half-feet rectangle, six feet deep. You will have memorized these dimensions by nightfall. The job is meant for four men. It is meant to take six hours. It will take you twelve.

ONE

They say the body is a temple; yours is a tomb. You have cultivated its marble architecture for years with every slash of a pocketknife, every hiss of a burn.

The first time you cut yourself, you were twelve years old. You were trying to open a portal to a new world through your wrists, but all you got was pain, blood and pain, and a rush of intense euphoria that told your brain, *This is good.*

Your mother found you, splayed out like Christ, and beat you with her wooden spoon and *How dare you!* and *What have you done!*

You didn't care. You had unlocked the secret of pain.

But you did care enough that next time, you slashed yourself across your hip, where your clothes would cover you and hide your blood-spotted secret.

TWO

When you were born, they opened you up and buried another child inside you. A lost child. A dead child. Then they stitched you back up and gave you his name. From then on, you were never just you. You were *we*. You were *us*. You were the amalgamation of hopes and dreams for two souls.

You loved it. You hated it. Carrying on someone's else's legacy at one, two, four, ten. Knowing that your achievements were his gains and your failures, a sign that you were never good enough to be his successor.

He wouldn't have come home late and made me worry.
He wouldn't have broken the lamp and tried to hide it.
Well he isn't here, Dad, Mom—what about me?
What about you?

THREE

The first time he hurt you, your "uncle," you were five and it was playtime and you were a pretty pretty princess, with the tiara and fairy wings and the rings, even the black ring nobody else liked but was special to you. You didn't know why, yet, you were drawn to the darkness of the world, didn't understand the boy stitched inside of you.

Come over here, your uncle said and, *Sit on my lap and tell me a story.*

And you did, you flew over to him on your wings without trepidation, because he was your uncle and you were invincible.

You told him the story of a pretty pretty princess living alone in a tower, and how she had a tea party, and how the woodland creatures saved her, and as you were doing this your uncle stuck his hands beneath your dress and touched you where you mama cleaned you in the bath, and it felt wrong and it felt good and you wanted to throw up.

What are you doing, uncle? you asked innocently. You were oh, so innocent.

Shh, he said, removing his hand. *This has to be our little secret.* Pinching you where your neck met your shoulder. *Shh.*

And you could feel your wings dissolve into sticky muck and turn to vapor, and the next time your "uncle" came, you tried to fly away but your wings were gone, and it was just you, and him, and the dim light of a moon-shaped lamp.

FOUR

It was eighth grade, and you were on the precipice of being popular. That is, you associated with popular people, and they told you how to change yourself. How to transform yourself into something acceptable to the world. With razors and sticks of eye makeup and lip color and special clothes, they redefined your being into a perfect chameleon.

Now you would be popular. *Now* you would be loved.

Shifting colors and clothes at will, you stalked behind the natural-born butterflies, glorying in their notice of you. Seen, for the first time, you found your insides meeting your outsides, glutting out into the world in diatribes of grief and agony that you'd never shared with anyone before.

It wasn't long before the head butterfly, your closest friend, came up to you one day and said with a smirk, *I think we need space. You vent too much. We can't be friends anymore.*

Three solitary sentences linked into one exultation of exclusion.

Your colors shifted to black and brown and gray and you watched as the butterfly flew away to the other butterflies. No one missed you. No one came to check on you.

You were alone now, holding their rejection in your hands like a seed.

And so you buried it deep, deep where it could implant and spread tendrils.

The boy? Was playing creepy crawlies with your insides.

FIVE

Some children love Christmas; you joyed in Halloween. While the peons were prying open their presents and pouting about what they got or didn't get, you delighted in the act of disguise. You were still a chameleon, but now you could shift your darks and drabs into any combination of colors you wanted. You could be ~~a princess never a princess or~~ an owl or the Grim Reaper himself or a goddess of the native wood. It didn't matter that no one else understood or appreciated your costumes. All that mattered was you were someone else for a night, and you were *powerful.*

It wasn't until you were twenty-three that you found your fellow darklings. You remember the first time someone invited you to the Carnival Miraculous. It was a theater of dreams, of daring, a spectacle sinister and sportive that only occurred during the month of Halloween. Debauchery ruled at this backwoods bacchanal where carnival rides and games were just opening fare, providing the amuse-bouche for darker delights. Surrounded by other chameleons, you danced and drank and gloried in the acrobatics and burlesque, and it was like the Carnival was your home.

But two years later, pandemic came, and the Carnival died too, and with it, the largest part of your soul.

SIX

Apparently, it's illegal to try to kill yourself.

You find this out on your eighteenth birthday, when you stuff your mouth full of lithium and Ativan and chase it with Jim Beam.

The boy in you is not quite quiet. He is sloppy seconds, slurring words—it's almost funny, it's almost sad, really.

You sit on the toilet for a while, growing woozy and faint, and then your stomach revolts and starts to spew onto the plastic you laid down to make the cleanup easier on your parents, who are sitting downstairs watching a network procedural crime drama so loud you can hear gunshots.

You pass in and out of consciousness, in, and out.

They find you—you wake up—in an hour, or two, when your father has to use the bathroom and they're out of toilet paper.

Why's the goddamned door locked?

Honey? Honey!

Your father kicks down the rickety door and they find you, marinating in your own shit and vomit, on the plastic-covered tile floor.

Call 911, we have to call 911.

You blink again, and the EMTs are there, shining lights in your eyes, asking what you've taken. Your throat hurts too much to speak, but they find the empty pill bottles on the side of the sink.

Let's get her on the stretcher, says one of the EMTs. *We need the doc to sign off on a psych hold.*

A psych hold? Dad cries. *My daughter is not crazy!*

Point-blank, he says, *Your daughter just tried to kill herself, sir.* Then he schleps you onto the stretcher, which he and his partner bang down the stairs and out into the chilly night.

The stars above you look luscious and ripe. You pluck one from the sky and pop it into your mouth, where it fizzes like lemon Pop Rocks, all the way to the hospital.

SEVEN

You were in Memphis watching horror movies when you got the call.

Oh, honey. Your dad. You didn't need her to finish the sentence.

Your dad, who'd been having heart problems. Your dad, who had refused to quit working because there was always more money to be made.

Your dad, who had gone into cardiac arrest on a ladder and then lain at the bottom, between the ladder and the house he was working on alone, for six hours before anyone found him.

Our dad, says the boy inside of you.

Shut up shut up shut up—you will not let him have this too.

You wear the same dress you wore to your aunt's funeral at the wake, the black one with the big transparent white flowers like ghosts, and you avoid your cousins and the few friends who could come. You want to see him first. You *need* to see him first.

While everyone else is in the receiving room, pouring wine and eating iced cookies, you head into the room with the casket. It's a beautiful piece, oak, maybe, with brass finishings. Your dad would have liked that.

Tiptoeing up like a child, you peer over the coffin. Your dad lies there, waxy and wrinkled, and he blinks at you. His tongue lolls out of his green-gray lips. You don't hesitate. You pull the shawl from your shoulders and you stuff it over his mouth and nose, and while tears stream down your face you press the shawl down harder, harder, until there is no more warmth of breath burning your hands, and your father's eyes are closed for good.

EIGHT

They say the French call orgasm "la petite mort," the little death. You had experienced many little deaths in your life, but you were twenty-five the first time it happened with another person. He was kind, nerdy, an ectomorph who gave off no alarm bells like some of the bulky boxer types who sometimes wooed you.

You had to be drunk first. It was the only way you could open up.

You didn't love him but, in the haze of Jack Daniel's and a few hits of weed, you were ready to profess everything to him. You told him your cherry-picked stories. Your "uncle." Your dead dad. Not enough to scare him off—unless he was too much of a pussy, in which case, good riddance—but enough to fabricate a false sense of closeness.

He held you, and his fingers dribbled down towards your crotch, and you stiffened at first, took another swig of Jack and Coke and let it blur your resistance away as he slid his fingers into you a little bit and then deeper.

You were not sure how, when, his fingers were replaced by his dick, but it hurt less than you had thought, or rather the pain was diffuse, throbbing throughout your body on a tide of weed, and you fucked for minutes or hours or somewhere in between and you even let him kiss you.

And as you fucked, you sucked the energy from his body through your skin, until you were golden and glowing and glorious and he was desiccated and asleep.

NINE

They said you never forget your first. You married yours. A precaution, perhaps? A preservative against loneliness. The boy stitched inside of you was no friend.

They said you looked beautiful that day, your chameleon skin painted in shades of white, gold, and silver. Surrounded by the cloying lily-stench of dying flowers, you made your way up a white aisle in a starry warehouse somewhere south of the river, where a nondenominational pastor and your ectomorph waited.

You felt like a ~~princess~~.

Your stomach clenched, vomit tickling the back of your throat. You'd already thrown up in the bridal suite bathroom.

You felt like a ~~princess~~.

No. No, you weren't going to let him have this too.

Like a *princess*.

With a slow step, you dragged your train down the aisle to the tinkling tones of Pachelbel's "Canon in D" because of course it was, you didn't care, and you stopped in front of your husband-to-be.

Do you take

Do you take

In sickness

In sickness

The vows carouseled through your brain, meaningless and trite.

'Til death

'Til death

You were already dying, the girl of you gone, replaced with the wingless woman who was to be this man's wife.

TEN

Dozens of little deaths later, and you could almost feel the quickening in your womb.

Fuck. You had never wanted this. Had used every means not to have this.

You know it's true when the test shows its cheery little plus sign that you hide deep in the trash, then take to the outside garbage where no one will see.

How was your day, darling? your husband asks.

Same shit, different day, you answer, a joke between you. He laughs. He kisses your nose.

You don't tell him about the quickening and the plus sign.

The next day, you drive to the next county over to find a clinic that will get you in discreetly. You're still not so far along, they say. They can use medication, they say.

You're used to poisoning yourself. You eat the abortifacients greedily and then sit in the motel room waiting for your insides to burn away like the embered ashes of paper lanterns on the Fourth of July.

ELEVEN

You are different after the abortion, as though the pills have scraped you hollow. As though even the boy inside you is gone.

You don't regret it. You don't feel sorrow or pain.

But whatever you felt for your husband, he who implanted you with the invasive species, is gone.

Gone.

What's wrong? he keeps asking you. Doesn't he see that every iteration fans the flames of your rage? Doesn't he see the deadness behind your eyes as you pour his nightly tea? Doesn't he wonder why it smells like almonds?

I'm fine, you assure him. *Drink up.*

He drinks.

You leave the room and go to your vanity. Somewhere downstairs, he is beginning to froth and convulse. For the first time in years, you are taking your pocketknife and trying to open a portal in your wrists to a better world.

But not all the way.

Not yet.

TWELVE

Well, he says when he opens the door, slicking back his thin, dyed hair. *I haven't seen you in years.*

You smirk, sultry, hoping the clingy dress you chose is to his taste. Perhaps only princess dresses on little girls are to his taste. *I was in the neighborhood,* you say. *Can I come in?*

He is unsuspicious, or else thinks he has the upper hand. He lets you in to that same old house with the shag carpet and deer skulls above the couch.

It doesn't escape you that he locks and chains the door.

The hairs on your arms stand up, but you breathe calm into your limbs and take his invitation to sit.

He offers you something to drink, something that could starch a collar. You take it. It doesn't matter. You won't be here long.

When he turns back from the bar cart, you have the gun pointed at his forehead. It wasn't hard to get one. You live in a red state.

Shit! he cries, dropping the glasses to shatter and spew the scent of liquor around the floor. *What are you doing? Put that away.*

No, you say. *Don't you worry. This will be our little secret.*

In TV shows, they always lose their courage because they wait.

You don't wait. You squeeze the trigger three times and hit him once through the meaty part of his chest. It's enough to get him on the floor where you can stand over him, executioner's style.

Any last words, motherfucker? you ask.

I—

You don't wait for him to finish speaking. You bury a bullet in his forehead.

———

Twelve hours later, your arms ache like they're about ready to fall off, and you stand at the bottom of one perfect grave.

Are we finished? you ask.

No, he says. *We've just begun.*

Poetry

FLESH GHOSTS

Andrew Kozma

Exhaustion wears me like a sleeve. I have been to Heaven
in my dreams, but wake to this damn leaden Earth.

Not even Hell. Not even Hell. What is salvation but an escape
from yourself? Before my father died, his toes turned black.

They blackened like too-ripe bananas. Before my father died,
we unplugged him from the wall. Then he died. He died,

and again I tell myself death is a transitional state, embodied
as long as the body lasts. The trees do it every year, a miracle

until the beetles bore through their hearts, the trees
crumpling like stale popcorn. Trees don't have souls. They live and die,

they burn to ash, they become the sky. My soul wears me
down with worry. I am the rock Sisyphus struggles up the hill.

And here, at the top, witness all the hills, every soul and body
cabled together. My father leaves the room. I plug myself in.

PENNY FOR THEM

Die Booth

CW: *childhood trauma, gay slurs*

"YOU LOOK DIFFERENT," Nan says.

"I'm forty-five, Nan," I say.

Squinting at me, she takes in my pigtails and my green nail polish and my handlebar moustache and nods decisively, as if the fact it's been a while is the only thing that's changed.

Nan looks the same. She's wearing a white cardigan with pearl buttons over a dress like a floral crimplene tabard, her fingers packed to the knuckles with rings. Her grey curls are done up all perfectly poofy like the Queen's, and she sounds like Lily Savage.

The Queen and Lily Savage both died this past twelve months. I still can't quite get my head around that.

Nan's house looks the same, too. There's an antimacassar on the arm of the sofa, and balanced on the antimacassar are the TV remote, the cordless phone, and a thick glass ashtray full of stubbed-out fag-ends, all lined up neat and tidy. The paint of the ceiling is a bit yellowed from smoke, but the nets at the window are snowy white. When I look carefully, I can see the painted-over eye-screws dotted around the doorframe, for the big old fake tree to be moored every Christmas with strings like guy-ropes to prevent it from toppling. When I look even more carefully, I can spot a single missed budgie poo stuck to the skirting board like a tiny Liquorice Allsort.

"You want a cuppa?" Nan asks. "We've got rabbit stew in the pantry."

I wasn't hungry until she mentioned food, but suddenly I am. The memory of rabbit legs floating in broth makes my stomach turn, though. I'm not sure how to navigate this politely.

"We could go out. Make it special."

I haven't been to my hometown in years. I have no idea what's even here anymore. Twitching the nets, I check for rain and see, where the square of scruffy grass in the middle of the close used to be, there now stands a Taco Bell restaurant, replacing the No Ball Games signs and abandoned footballs.

I know it's a Taco Bell from the red neon that spells out Taco Bell with a flashing sign that mimics a bell ringing, somehow bright even in the dull English daylight. Everything else about it blends in, though, to the dowdy Northern terraces and semis edging the close: low, red-tiled roof and grey bricks, a bit defeated-looking. "We could go to Taco Bell."

"What's a Taco Bell, then?" Nan asks, as if she's not looked out of the window since this shiny new fast-food joint manifested on the green. I let it go.

"It's like McDonald's, but it sells tacos." This is pretty much the sum of my understanding of the place.

Nan doesn't even blink. "What's a McDonald's?"

When are we? I say, "A fast-food place, sells hamburgers."

And Nan says, "Ohhhh, the Wimpy."

"Yeah. Like Wimpy, but tacos."

"What's a taco, then?" Nan asks.

I think. "Like a mince pancake?" I hazard.

Nan raises her feathery eyebrows and gives an impressed little nod. She looks a bit surprised too, like she wasn't expecting something so appetising. "Well, what are we waiting for? Let's get going, then."

I wait, as she puts on her camel coat with the gold chained Mizpah brooch on the lapel, changes out of her slippers, and checks that her purse is in her handbag. We go out the back door and down the entry, past the little utility room where the fridge and the washing machine live. It's even worse than I remember, now I'm tall enough to have to duck beneath the spider-garlanded roof. Nan unlocks the side gate, then locks it behind us. The air outside feels staticky, like we're due a storm, but there's not a cloud in the magnet-coloured sky. Across the road, the Taco Bell sign winks, come-hither.

"This is nice, isn't it?" Nan says. We're installed opposite one another in a diner-style booth, with cherry-red pleather upholstery and matching red piping around the curved edges of the glossy yellow tabletop. It makes me think of hot dogs—mustard and ketchup. The lamp overhead is long and low like the kind you see in pool halls. There's a vase in the centre of the table, chrome as a flying saucer, filled with purple hyacinths and baby's breath. She balances her folded arms on her handbag, which is resting on her lap, and looks around. She hasn't taken her coat off. I shake out of my jacket and fold it on the seat beside me, and after a minute, Nan sets her bag next to her, closest to the wall. She keeps her coat on.

"It's all right, yeah." They're piping in some cheesy old pop, and I can recite every lyric but not for the life of me remember the artist. Rancid nostalgia fists my guts. Too many happy songs make me sad now. I want the past, but when I reach for it, like tearing down a sun-faded poster, it comes apart in my hands. I don't think it was ever what I wanted. I don't think it was ever even real. I look around, too. "I can't see any menus." But a server wearing a white apron and a white smile is approaching our table.

"Would you like popcorn shrimp?" the server asks. He has very attentive eyebrows.

"What's popcorn shrimp when it's at home?" Nan says. She gets her fags out of her bag and I'm about to say something about the smoking ban. But then I remember the smoking ban probably hasn't happened yet.

"I reckon." I think of popcorn chicken. "It's shrimp in like, breadcrumbs. Or batter. Then they fry it."

"We used to get shrimp at New Brighton on the front. Fresh caught that day. They were beautiful." She enunciates every syllable for emphasis, bee-you-ti-full, exhaling a smoky breath and tapping her ash into the pressed metal ashtray that was suddenly there all along on the bright laminate tabletop.

I remember the last time I got seaside seafood. I think it was at Parkgate. I was about seventeen and it was cockles in a paper cup with a plastic chip fork and it had me sprinting in and out of the loo right through that night's episode of *The X-Files*. They used to sell them in the pub as well, back then, a guy coming round with a tray full of seafood like that's what teenagers want with a pint. We called him the Fishy Man. *Hey, Fishy Man, get your fish away from me.* Him and the guy who sold single plastic-wrapped red roses from a bucket. *Boys, buy a rose for your lady.* Those paper cups make me think of medicine doses, now. I push the thought away. The next one crowds in to take its place, rattling like a bottle on a production line.

The night before my grandad died, he'd given me a handful of change to spend. Silvers and coppers. For argument's sake, twenty-three p. The day after, he was gone. Nan had woken up next to him in the morning, heart attacked. The perfect fairy-tale death you fantasise about—passing away peacefully in your sleep. Well, perfect for him, anyway. My mum said gravely to me, "You must never spend that money." I put it… somewhere. I was eight.

"That'll be twenty-three pence, please," the server says, sunshinely. When I look in my wallet, none of my bank cards are there, but there's the exact change, in '80s money, the coins big and thick, with the Queen's face all young and glam.

"It's what he would've wanted," Nan says, like she knows what I'm thinking. And it's true. I know he'd rather me have spent it on snacks than kept it stashed away until it became un-legal tender, even the memory faded. People want things to stay the same. But things can't stay the same. That's the only certainty in life.

I wish I knew what else he'd rather. I think about him laughing at ballet dancers on telly, and tiny me laughing along with him. "Who's the poofter with the big packet?" That one sticks in my head, the exact intonation he'd use at the budgie. "Who's a pretty boy, then? Who's a little bugger?"

"I am," the budgie would reply, in a voice like radio static.

I'm named after him. My grandad, not the budgie. *Who's a pretty boy, then. Who's a little bugger.*

I am.

These memories are outdated. If he'd lived long enough to see me grow up, maybe he'd have changed, maybe he wouldn't. I can't reconcile those aspic words with my grandad who (I know. I'm told. I choose to believe.) loved me. When you're a kid, people tell you how you feel. And you don't know any better, so you just believe them. You like a girl character? Oooh, you fancy her! You like a boy character? You want to be like him when you grow up! Vice-versa. Whatever. Grown-ups could have told me pink was blue when I was little and I'd have just accepted it and repeated it back. So I never knew why things felt off, like I'd sidestepped a millimetre outside of myself and was constantly hovering to catch up, laughing along with Grandad at that queer little man on *Are You Being Served?*

Even though we're frozen in time at our final moment (Leave an impression! Make it count!), if it had all played out to this point, there's a chance it would still be okay. The server is still standing there, smiling patiently. I pass the coins over, like Charon's obol. The dead stay dead. Until they don't.

Nan nudges me with her elbow. "What are you getting?"

Older, I think. Sadder. "Huh?"

"To eat!" Nan looks between me and the server and gives him a twinkly smile.

"Oh. Yeah. Ah." What did I just pay for while I wasn't paying attention? "Tacos, I guess?" There are probably a dozen different variations on tacos on the menu. The server just smiles, as if he understands exactly what I need. He nods, turns with a flourish, and walks away.

Nan watches him leave, with mild interest. "Do you think he's a bit...?" She doesn't do the camp hand gesture, but the tone is enough, so familiar it's almost, in a weird, sick way, nostalgic.

"You know *I'm* a bit?" I say.

Nan rolls her eyes. "I'm not daft."

I think I knew that she knew. But it still creeps through me like anaesthetic, numbing my lips and freezing my tongue. She says, "You know I've been dead for—what is it, nearly forty years, now?"

I feel dead, too. I will my tongue to move. "I know, Nan."

"Time doesn't half fly."

It does. Even when you're not having fun, it does. I feel half-here, half-somewhere, drifting in the space in between the knowing and not-knowing. Send help: I've fallen asleep and I can't get up. "And what do you, you know. Think. About it? Me?" I ask her.

Nan slides me an amused look. "What do you care what a dead lady thinks?"

That's the bones of it, isn't it? Why *do* I care? "Because I don't want you to hate me. To have hated me. To hate who I became. Who I am. Who I will be." Who I always was, it just took me a while to understand it, piecing together clues and impulses like some experimental escape room in the dark. Waiting for someone to tell me I'm not wrong, not sick, not a freak. Waiting for some kind of permission from God knows who, or who-knows's God. Or grandmother.

"I don't hate you, chuck." Nan says.

"But *would* you have hated me?" I don't say, *back then or, if you hadn't died,* but she seems to understand.

"Now, how can I answer that? Nobody can tell what might have been, if things were different," Nan says. Then, "But no. I wouldn't have hated you. I wouldn't ever have hated you."

I nod, wondering if I'm going to cry. I find it hard to, these days. Do I want her to love me, or do I want me to love me? I wipe my eyes with my fingertips anyway.

"That's posh," Nan says, changing the subject. She's looking at the ring with the big garnet on my first finger. She takes my hand and I suddenly feel like, yes, I might cry, actually.

"You can have it," I blurt out. I have the sudden clear memory of loving a turquoise costume ring of hers, and her giving it to me, far too big for my tiny kid fingers. She's probably the reason I developed a socially inappropriate jewellery addiction.

Reading my mind again, she says, "Looks better on you, love. You always did like your tranklements."

"So did you." The past tense hovers over us. The hour is getting late. I wonder when Taco Bell closes, whenever we are. Do they shoo folk out at six, or like old-fashioned last orders at eleven—you don't have to go home, but you can't stay here. Is it open all night, like a drive-thru, or a diner in a Tom Waits song?

I don't want to go home. But I can't stay here.

"We should go." I say.

Nan tuts. "I haven't had my taco yet." But I know she agrees. She's reaching for her handbag to tuck her cigarettes back inside.

The overhead light seems to dim, reflecting yellow in the chrome of the little vase in front of me.

I don't like cut flowers. They make me feel sad. But I'm suddenly sad that no boy is ever gonna buy me a cellophane rose from a bucket in a pub. I'm sad for all the might-have-beens and missed tricks and opportunities lost and stolen. I'm sad for the might-bes and the maybes and the not-yets, too. Perhaps I'm just sad. These flowers, though—I pluck a jaunty stalk of hyacinth out of the vase—they're never going to wilt. Leaning across the table, I gesture to Nan.

"Instead of the taco. A souvenir from home." I thread the flower into the buttonhole on her lapel, next to the Mizpah brooch.

I try to dig a space in amongst the sad for another feeling to take root.

Nan looks down at the purple petals, then at me, and I catch myself trying to memorise the look, and stop myself sternly. Live in the now. "Penny for your thoughts?" she asks.

I smile at her. Live, now. "They're worth a lot more than that," I say.

Fiction

THE WANDERER

C. T. Muchemwa

MY SON does not know that I am dead because he is far from home wandering. So when I die, lying on my grass mat, I am surrounded by my dead wife's relatives, all of them peering at me with an impatient look.

One of them says to me, "Just let go. Dying is like falling."

But he is wrong. For dying is more like sinking. Even though I hold on stubbornly to life, I feel myself sinking. I call out my son's name one final time, "Vambe."

Dying is standing in a river watching the water that was around your ankles rising, while the riverbed under your feet steadily drops. And the last thought I have, just before the water closes over my head, is wondering who it is who will tell my son that I am dead.

After I die, my spirit is in the wilderness. I am in a dark forest and all around me there are wandering spirits. Everywhere I look, I see the dead. Some of them watch silently, as if they are waiting for their time when they will be called out of the wilderness and back home. Others moan in fear, horrified by all the death they see. Others weep for the lives they can never return to. But the ones that disturb me the most are the ones who wail. They are dark shadows, like they have been wandering so long that they have lost their human shape. And they wail endlessly as I feel them brush past me in a futile search for a way home. Futile because none of us can make it home on our own.

The only way home is if our families perform the kurova guva ceremony to call our spirits home. For a year, we each must wander. Then the ceremony happens and our spirits can return to the family homestead to join the ancestors and watch over our descendants for eternity. But what happens to those who are never called home? What happens to those who have no one to perform the kurova guva for them? Are they these shadows that wail unendingly? The questions threaten to overwhelm me. And in the wilderness, I begin to panic.

Everywhere, I see these restless spirits who have never been called home. I see the spirits of the abandoned, people who had illnesses, physical deformities or disabilities that their families did not want passed on to the next generation, so they buried them far away and never called their spirit home. I see the spirits of those who died far from home, soldiers, merchants, and hunters who fell where no one knew them, and no one would remember where they were buried. But it's the spirits of the forgotten that alarm me the most. People who were loved, and wander in the wilderness wondering why their people do not call them home.

My son does not know that I am dead. So how can he ever have a kurova guva ceremony for me? I ask myself this question and know immediately that I must find him. He does not know I am dead because he has been away from home for five years now. Vambe left home at nineteen years old in search of adventure. He did not think about leaving his father at home alone. He did not think about his responsibilities. He only thought of the horizon and finding out what was beyond it. So he carried his bow and arrow and a few things in his animal skin bag, then set out. When I was alive, I had no idea where he was, but now that I am dead, I am surprised by how quickly I find him. As I turn my mind to him in the fog of wilderness, a light appears on the edge. I walk towards it. I walk for what feels like weeks towards the growing beacon, and I persevere because I know I will find my son.

What I expect to see at the end of the light is a village, clusters of small huts made of mud, wood, and straw. But what I find is a large stone city filled with structures built from perfectly stacked granite blocks. It is a bustling place with men and women hurrying along as they do their Mambo's bidding. A place as elaborate as this must be the seat of a mighty ruler. Large men wearing buck hides and holding large spears stand guard at the city entrance, and floating behind them is an army of mudzimu barring my entry. These ancestral spirits are not like the spirits in the wilderness. For one thing, I can see them clearly. For another, they speak to each other. And right now, they are speaking about me.

"Who is this wanderer?" the spirit of an old man says.

"I do not recognize him," another answers.

"You must not let him in," the old man says.

The spirits glare at me and some begin to stand in a line, barring entry into the city.

"Wait. He feels familiar," says the spirit of a middle-aged woman with a baby suckling from her breast. "I feel like I know him, even though he is obscured in darkness." She squints at me, as if trying to penetrate a cloud around me. "I know who he feels like. He feels like the foreigner."

And just like that, they let their guard down. Immediately, they understand what I am doing here, that my son drew me to him, and even in death I had no choice but to come.

As I wander the stone city, I wonder how my Vambe found his way here. What can possibly be making him linger in this place instead of returning home to his baba? The answer, of course, is a woman. I find Vambe sitting on a rocky outcrop, watching a group of women below who laugh as they braid each other's hair. The markings on their brown hide skirts identify them as members of the Mambo's family. There are five of them, all young, beautiful maidens, but it is obvious which one has caught Vambe's eye. The most beautiful of them all. She is easily the shortest of them, yet she still stands out. And when she smiles...when she smiles... Any man who saw her would tell you that when she smiles, it is like the first gulp of water from a cold river after a long journey; it brings life to parts of you that you didn't even know were dying. But on

Vambe's face it is clear that for him, when she smiles there is absolutely nothing else that matters.

In the days that follow, I discover that the woman is the eldest daughter of the Mambo of the city. I wonder where my child ever found the audacity to fall in love with a princess. For in love they are.

For weeks, I watch Vambe manufacturing meetings with the princess. He volunteers to serve as a guard when she leaves the city with the other maidens in search of herbs. And at night, she sneaks out of her hut, and they meet by the river. And there they sit, hand in hand, talking about the future that they dream of. An impossible future, for the Mambo will never let his daughter marry a poor foreigner.

———

My son does not know that I am dead, but sometimes I think he feels me. I think he senses that I am near. When he walks back to the warriors' barracks after his meetings with the princess, I think he senses me following in his footsteps. He turns back quickly, looking intently, but he stares right through me, face wrinkled in confusion. I am right here, but he cannot see me. I plead with him to go home, but he cannot hear me. How will he ever learn that he needs to save me? On nights like those, I cannot bear to watch him sleep peacefully when I am facing oblivion. On nights like those, I wander around the city. I encounter the mudzimu of this place, but none of them speak to me. They watch me with pity as I drift past them, then they whisper behind my back. Are they wondering just like I am how much longer my spirit will retain its shape, or when I will begin to fade to shadow?

———

My son does not know that I am dead, so he spends his days amongst the warriors of the stone city, trying to ingratiate himself with the King. Whatever unpleasant task is required, Vambe volunteers. He searches for firewood with the young boys. He helps the female servants bring water from the river to the cooking place. When the travelling merchants at the market get overexcited, he is there to bring them back in line. And when it is time to fight, he is always at the front. The warriors of this place favour spears as weapons, but my son has always carried his bow and arrows. And he is so efficient with his weapons of choice that they call him Chirashamihwa, one who throws needles the way that porcupines do. When the men set out to hunt, it is always his arrow that brings the beasts down. When they return, it is his name the women sing. The months go by, and Vambe steadily works his way into the Mambo's inner circle. He is known throughout the stone city as a problem solver. But a new problem is looming that even my Vambe cannot solve. A drought is deepening, water is dwindling, and each time the men set out on a hunt, they have to go farther and farther to find the animals. The entire city is at risk of starvation.

So, one day, the Mambo calls a special meeting for his warriors, and I follow Vambe as he walks to a meeting that he was not invited to.

When the Mambo sees him, he says "Chirashamihwa, why are you here? You may be brave, and you have helped where you can. But you are still a foreigner. I cannot ask you to risk your life for people who aren't your own."

"Mambo, I am your servant," Vambe says. "Give me your orders and I will go." And so, my Vambe sits down and joins the other warriors, awaiting the Mambo's commands. The Mambo looks at his men with a worried look on his face. He lets out a big sigh before he finally speaks.

"I do not have to tell you the problems that face this city," the Mambo says. "Look at this land. All that was once green now lies dying of thirst under the unforgiving sun. Our ancestors have deserted this land. Maybe it is time we did too. But I don't want to leave. This is the only home we all have ever known, but I know to remain here would be to condemn my people to die. So, I challenge each of you to go out in search of water. And whoever brings us water can have my daughter's hand in marriage. Go. Go now. Find me water. Save my people."

My son does not know that I am dead, so when he makes his prayers to his ancestors to guide him on his way, he does not include me. He calls on my father, and my grandfather, and the ancestors who came before them. I know they hear him because they are not in the wilderness like I am. Their spirits were called home, and he will always be able to find them. Hearing him recite the long line of fathers makes me afraid once again. How long will I be able to see my son and hear him before the wilderness swallows me entirely? I listen as he asks for protection and guidance. I listen as he tells them about this woman he adores. I listen as he begs them to help him secure his wife. And the following morning, before the rooster crows, he sets out with dozens of other men. They split into groups and begin their search, each man determined to claim the title of being the Mambo's son-in-law.

My son does not know that I am dead. Perhaps if he did, he would abandon this quest and go back to find my grave. Then finally my kurova guva ceremony would be held. As I watch him and the other young men hunting for water, I dream about my kurova guva ceremony. I imagine the people gathering by my grave. I see them bringing sadza, beer, and my favourite snuff. They slaughter a cow, and they spend the night singing and dancing in the yard. And in the morning, my son leads them back to my grave, and there, they fetch my spirit. They say "We are calling you back home. You do not need to live in the wilderness any longer." And finally, *finally,* my spirit will be able to join my ancestors. But these are only dreams, and that future seems to be fading now. My son has no intention of turning back.

The warriors wander for days, and steadily, one by one, they start to turn back. The sun is too strong, the food dwindles, and they begin to give up. They give up until it is only Vambe who remains. Even though he is now alone, he continues his search for water. The stubbornness that made him leave home in the first place propels him now. He has decided that he will find this water. He has decided that he will marry this woman. So, he searches, surging forward even though his feet hurt, his back aches, and his skin begins to pinch from the pain of the sun beating down on it relentlessly. He continues even as he begins to weaken.

And as Vambe gets weaker, the line between life and death blurs. I lie beside him as he sleeps, and sometimes I am able to enter his dreams. In his dreams, I try to speak to him, but he cannot understand me. My presence just seems to fluster him. So as the days proceed, I choose instead to lie and watch the stars while he sleeps. I remember the days after his mother died, when Vambe and I made the trek to her people in search of safety. When we would rest at night, I couldn't sleep. I needed to stay awake to keep my son safe. So I would lie next to him, listening to his steady breathing. I would look at the stars. They looked so bright. And something about the vastness of the sky and the multitude of stars that stretched across the universe reminded me about just how small a part I was in it. In those moments when everything else fell into insignificance in comparison to the immensity of the night sky, that very feeling of futility left me feeling completely stripped down to the things that mattered to me most. And that thing for me was Vambe and finding a place that we could call home.

Now I watch the sky, and I know that the thing that matters most to me is still my son. I cannot help but wonder what Vambe thinks of when he looks at the night sky. When he is forced to face just how small and insignificant he is, what are the things that still hold meaning? Does he wonder about me and the people he left behind? Or does he only think about the young woman who has captured his heart and the life that he will build with her? Does he ever look back, or does he only think about the future and the legacy he wants to leave?

My son does not know that I am dead, so when his thirst starts to make him delirious, he calls to his dead mother. He falls to his knees and begins to crawl in the grass as he begs his mother to save him. And like a mirage, a thicket of trees appears on the horizon. He drags himself towards the trees. Slowly, he reaches his goal. And in this place, there is a pool of water. In any other circumstance, Vambe would know immediately that this is a holy place. He would know the risks of disturbing the water. But because he is in the state he is in, all he sees is water and the end of his thirst. He falls to his knees, and he leans down, as he drinks greedily.

"You'll choke if you keep drinking like a drunk elephant," I say.

Vambe stiffens as if a noise has startled him. At the exact same time, I feel a shift. Like a veil has fallen away.

Vambe lifts his head in my direction. He says "Baba?"

I am momentarily frozen. Did he hear me? I do not know what to do. My son calling for "Baba" again startles me out of my shock. I realise that he is not looking through me. He is looking at me. My son can see me.

"Baba, how can you be here?" Vambe says. "You were alive when I left you."

"Mwanangu, my precious son, I am with you always."

"Baba, you have to help me."

"My son…" I begin to say, but then I pause. The moment feels so important, and I am overwhelmed by the worry that I have this one chance to get it absolutely right. But Vambe has ideas of his own. He keeps talking, even as I struggle to find the words.

Vambe says, "Now that you are gone, I am alone. Help me win this woman I love so I can have a family again."

I want to tell him to abandon this quest. I want to tell him he needs to go home. I want to tell him he needs to do the kurova guva ceremony so that I can join my ancestors. But I cannot get a word in edgewise. I am trying to get my son to think about where he comes from, his responsibilities to the past, but the only thing in his mind is the future. The only thing on his mind is this woman that he is building every dream upon. And I know I have to let him go.

So, I tell him where the water is.

I have always known where the water is. I knew almost as soon as I arrived in the city on that very first day. Untethered from the physical body and its distractions, the spirit becomes overly aware of the earth and how it moves. I could sense the water under the earth. An ancient river that is now hemmed in by rock, aggressively trying to find its way out. I always knew where the water was. There in the middle of the Mambo's meeting place. All Vambe needs to do is use his arrows to free it.

And the final thing I tell my son before he turns away from the pool is "Go and claim your wife."

My son now knows that I am dead, but all he can think about is that he now knows what he needs to be able to marry the princess. His love and desire propel him across the land, and he finishes the journey in just three days. He finds the entire city gathered in the meeting place. There is an air of mourning. The Mambo is announcing how they must all head north in search of better land and water. All the children are silent, and some women are weeping quietly. Vambe hurtles through the crowd and straight to the Mambo.

"I know where the water is. I will save my people."

"Where?" asks the Mambo says incredulously.

"Right here!" Vambe says.

Vambe now faces the large rock in the meeting place. The people all look at him. He takes out his bow and arrow, takes aim and shoots. His arrow hits the rock with a slight tap and falls tamely to the ground. A few people laugh. He tries another arrow with the same results. The people begin to leave the meeting area saying that the sun has gotten to the foreigner's head. He tries a third time and still no water.

The Mambo looks at him disappointedly and says, "I expected more from you." He walks away with the few remaining people and leaves Vambe alone. My son cannot understand. He looks around in confusion, almost as if he is waiting for me to appear and explain. I want to tell him to try again. But I cannot. His shoulders fall, and he looks at the rock dejectedly as if surveying the gravestone of his dreams.

Then a gentle voice says to him, "Try again, Chirashamihwa. A porcupine leaves many quills in the lion's face." He looks up and realizes that one person is still watching him. There stands the princess, a few steps away with an encouraging smile. "Try again."

He picks up his bow and arrows and sets aim again and shoots a fourth time at the stubborn rock, but still nothing. Not wanting to disappoint the princess, he gets ready to shoot again, stringing his bow, but before he can let the arrow go, the ground begins to tremble. Then there is a loud cracking sound. The rock breaks in two and water gushes out, drenching Vambe and the princess.

The water spouts out as it showers over the pair. The noise summons the people who all scream with joy at the sight of water. Some begin to dance. Others get on their knees and begin to praise and thank Mwari. Others still run to find containers for the water. And in the middle of it all, Vambe and the princess stand, staring at each other, speechless, as if overwhelmed by the realisation that what had once felt like an impossible dream of being together is really going to come true. They look at each other, water droplets sparkling in the sun. And in those drops, I see…the future. I see Vambe's son, and his son, and his sons' sons. I see the homes they will build. I see the wives they will marry. I see the daughters they will treasure. And I see them all, standing tall and proudly as they carry their ancestor's name: Chirashamihwa, mukwasha waMambo, Chikandamina weshanu uri pauta.

I see my descendants, and I feel the ties that bind me to my son loosening. The light dims. The sound stops. And once again, I am sinking. I am sinking like I did when I died. Sinking away from my son, sinking away from this city, and sinking away from the world. I sink into darkness, into the void where I know I will never be able to leave. I wander in the wilderness forever so that my son's wandering can end.

Fiction

FRACTIONATED DOSES DON'T QUENCH THE THIRST OF THOSE WHO KNEW THE WHOLE

Le Werner

ANOTHER CADAVER on the table. Another lot of spirits for a funeral.

Dona Zelma had been fermenting under the sun for more than a decade. Retired from her job and children, she spent most of her time sitting on her porch, watching life drain from her pores into the gutters of the tiny town lodged between river and sea, the one that hid behind the ocean-green tanks of its proud distillery.

The alcoholic air hid the smell of sun-dried meat until a couple days later. The boys from the mill found Dona Zelma in her chair, still rocking. They thought it was odd when she didn't wave as they crossed the dirt road by her farm, a routine of every morning. She was plopped on the Distiller's table in the same bleached clothes, with a box of anything they found in her house as a side.

The Distiller, weary, asked what they knew of her. Family? Friends? Deeds? They knew she liked her porch and to wave. With failing patience, she told them to scour the town for anyone that could consider Dona Zelma a loved one.

Alone with the body, there was much to be done by the Distiller before it could be drunk at the funeral, and yet not enough she could arrange herself. The fermenting wasn't supervised as it was practice, when the spirits-to-be got themselves anchored to hospital beds. There were no rites, no parting words or tears or emotions. Just a dried old lady, much akin to a gecko in the winter.

The box of belongings wasn't great cachaça material, either. A worn dog collar, small and far too old for it to still have a neck attached. Colorless photos of beachgoers, in none of which was

Dona Zelma present. A cookbook where half the recipes were printed from some website.

There was, however, the recipe for an onion pie, noted in the smallest cursive. A memory in yellowed paper. The Distiller cut it from the book and threw it into the fluid in the large copper tub. Soon the yeast made some of it come loose: a party and a full house, a busy kitchen, and a comforting dish all bobbed in the foamy surface.

In the late afternoon, as the Distiller bathed the remains of Dona Zelma, the Daughter Who Stayed came in to see the body. Knowledge of the old woman's death travelled by word of mouth until it reached her, the night baker from the Pão Nobre bakery at the end of the street.

At first, she didn't believe it was her Zelma. The mother was there on the porch, a postcard of the town, and a looming shadow over her children, most which had slipped out into the world. The Baker thought one day she would be able to walk around her mother's shade and find her smiling in the light. Now that hope was also going into the tub.

The Daughter kneeled by the vessel. The Distiller offered to hold her hair while she let all out, but the Daughter would rather avoid the touch of the woman from the tanks. The corpse brewer had a light in her eyes while watching the emission process, something like a forbidden hunger.

The words of the Daughter flew. A leakage turned into a flood, of kissed bruises and slaps, exaltation and humiliation, cooperation and competition, tempers and comfort. With a last choked spit, she gave enough material for a funeral. A metallic adjective, "unapologetic," floated for a moment before sinking to the bottom.

The Distiller asked if the Daughter wanted to watch the process. The answer was an obligatory yes.

Dona Zelma's corpse was lowered into the tub as if being put to sleep. The lid was fixed over it, and the heat raised. The vapors released were then pushed through cool pipes, and the resulting liquid repeated the process, again and again, thirteen times until the necessary purity was reached.

By then, it was already morning.

———————

The eulogies of the priest and the mayor had no words against the reputation of Dona Zelma. In truth, they praised her sense of community and dedication to her family, while brandishing cups of the cachaça the deceased was made into. A strong and rich beverage with notes of love and affection combined with noble self-sacrifice. The drink was approved by the entire town, whether they knew and liked Dona Zelma or not.

The Daughter couldn't drink it. Her eyes were fixed on the urn in the middle of the chapel, the one she helped the Distiller fill. The main vessel had the remains from the tub, which were mostly the heavy things we all drag along: guts, metabolism, and effluvia. The thirteen smaller urns came from each step, something of Dona Zelma only the Daughter could touch.

Into these subsequent distillations came loose the leaded assumptions let run bitter over the years, and the salts of feelings left unsaid. One could hear the smashing and the shouting, smell the tears and forced excuses.

The Distiller approached the Daughter, but not to comfort. She told the Daughter that she should taste the drink, for all its flavors were true, as much as they felt like lies. The Daughter spilled her dose on the ground, left it for the saints or the devil to give their approval.

She then asked the Distiller a simple question: Was that look in her eyes envy? Did the Distiller know she wouldn't taste as good in her own funeral?

The Distiller answered with a pained laugh that she spent too long hidden under the shadow of her tanks to taste like anything. Nothing latches her to the earth, good or bad. When her time arrives, she won't be distilled, she will sublimate; and along with her will disappear the tired tradition of drinking up the dead.

Poetry

THE INTERROGATION OF SAINT WINIFRED

Caroline Shea

GET UP. TELL IT.

up from the dark faces swim   puckered thread I'm jammed
& can't unstick   bodied again   a self
in stark relief against the universe   a creature of want
& need   it hurts to be
an I

TELL IT STRAIGHT. QUIT TRYING TO MAKE IT PRETTY.

fine   I died   I left   I went somewhere else

WHERE DID YOU GO?

an elsewhere an absence an abscess
does it matter what I call it
it was quiet there   it stripped me to the bone
I had no words   I had no meat

TELL IT FROM THE BEGINNING.

no such thing

TRY.

my mother says when I was born
I whispered my name in her ear
speech broke through   bloodied my gums

WHO KILLED YOU?

a man a man   like any other   do the dead care

YOU AREN'T DEAD. NOT ANYMORE.

I still speak their tongue

DO YOU FORGIVE HIM?

I lack that muscle

DID IT HURT?

you always ask that   do you think death a picnic
of course it hurt

DYING?

yes but   coming back was worse
my maiden's head stitched to a mangled neck
         a well sprung from
my blood I could hear it hum
in time with my heart
my viscera missed me

WHY DID HE KILL YOU?

oh he could never bear any beauty
he couldn't keep   I planned to marry God
to gift myself a life unfettered   (the divine
a rather absent lord&master)

when I would not open for him   he opened
me   made a door   my mouth dripped
curses

WHAT HAPPENED THEN?

the earth ate him whole   I'm told
they prayed me back to life   that I woke like a princess
lithe & unruffled   birds in my hair

AND NOW?

the spring where I fell runs red   smells of incense and decay
        wounds I touch
knit shut I pull the dead
from the grave   tell them get up get up
draw speech from their tongues   I teach them to live
again   to carry death with them
like pilgrims   to tell the story to anyone
        who asks

WHAT HAPPENS WHEN YOU TELL IT?

I live & live & live again

AUTHOR BIOS

JUSTIN CRUZANA is a poetry editor for *HaluHalo Journal*. His recent works have appeared in the Ateneo Art Gallery website, Stone of Madness Press, *B O D Y*, and *TLDTD*.

MARIA HASKINS is a Swedish-Canadian writer and reviewer of speculative fiction. Currently, she's located just outside Vancouver with two kids, a husband, a snake, several noisy birds, and a very large black dog. Her work is available in the short story collections *Wolves & Girls* and *Six Dreams About the Train*. She is an Aurora Awards nominee and an Ignyte Awards nominee. Maria's work has appeared in several publications and anthologies, including *Best Horror of the Year, Nightmare, Lightspeed, Interzone, Black Static, Fireside, Shimmer, Pseudo-Pod, Beneath Ceaseless Skies*, and elsewhere. Since 2016, she writes a monthly speculative short fiction roundup that is currently published at Maria's Reading. She also writes a quarterly short fiction column at *Strange Horizons*.

JOSHUA LIM is a writer of speculative fiction from Klang, Malaysia. His work is published or forthcoming in *Fantasy Magazine, PodCastle, The Deadlands, The Dark, Reader Beware,* and in various anthologies across the US, UK, and Malaysia. He is currently a medical student who spends too much time writing stories instead of studying. Find him at joshualimwriter.wordpress.com or on Instagram @joshualimwriter.

GUAN UN is an Australian-Chinese writer based in Sydney, who is often writing about tricksters when he's not writing about dead whales. His work has been featured in *Year's Best Fantasy Vol. 2, LeVar Burton Reads, Strange Horizons,* and more. He lives with his family, too many keyboards, and a dog named after a tiger. Find him on Bluesky (@thisisguan.bsky.social) or guanun.com.

ISHITA BASU MALLIK is a visual artist/cartoonist/poet based in Kolkata, India. She has been previously published in *ANMLY, Komikaze, SUSPECT,* and elsewhere, and recently received a Pushcart Prize nomination. In 2011, she won the Toto Funds the Arts award for Creative Writing in English. Ishita shares artwork irregularly on instagram @sunbornart.

PENELOPE K. PARKER is currently pursuing her BFA in writing & publishing at Emerson College in Boston, MA. Her work can be found on *Memoir Mixtapes* and in Emerson's *Concrete Literary Magazine.* Most days, she can be found either hiking in the mountains or hunched over at her desk. She's a native New Yorker, but spent the past summer with a travel writing group in Europe. Yes, she knows her name is an alliteration, and no, she isn't related to Peter Parker. Find her on Instagram as @penelopekparker.

C. J. SUBKO is a dreamer and a dabbler. She has a PhD in Clinical Psychology from Michigan State University and a BA in Psychology and English from the University of Notre Dame, which makes her highly qualified to think too much. Her short fiction publications include *Spindle House, Crow & Cross Keys, Skin, The Other Stories* podcast, *Cold Signal, Die Laughing, Small Wonders,* and *Penumbric Speculative Fiction.* She is a member of the HWA and SFWA. Her novels are represented by Maria Brannan at Greyhound Literary Agency. She can be found at www.cjsubko.com.

ANDREW KOZMA'S poems appear in *Rogue Agent, Redactions,* and *Contemporary Verse 2,* while his fiction appears in *Apex,* ergot, and *Seize the Press*. His first book of poems, *City of Regret*, won the Zone 3 First Book Award, and his second book, *Orphanotrophia*, was published in 2021 by Cobalt Press. You can find him on Bluesky at @thedrellum.bsky.social and visit his website at www.andrewkozma.net.

DIE BOOTH likes wild beaches and exploring dark places. When not writing, he DJs alongside his boyfriend at Last Rites—the best (and only) goth club in Chester, UK. His prize-winning work has featured in publications from Brigid's Gate Press, Egaeus Press, Flame Tree Publishing, Sans PRESS, Neon Hemlock, and many more. *Cool S*, a cursed novella, is out now. *365 Lies*, a collection of one flash fiction for every day of the year with all proceeds going to the MNDA, and the short story collections *My Glass is Runn* and *Making Friends* (and other fictions) are also available online, along with his novel *Spirit Houses*. He is currently working on a queer folk-horror novella. You can find out more about his writing at diebooth.wordpress .com or say hi on Instagram @dieboothwrites or Bluesky @diebooth.bsky.social.

C. T. MUCHEMWA is a Zimbabwean writer currently living in Canada. She was a 2022 recipient of the Morland African Writing Scholarship. Her debut short story collection, *Who Will Bury You and Other Stories*, was published in 2024 by House of Anansi Press.

LE WERNER (she/they) is a writer, translator, and editor from Curitiba, Brazil. Their short stories in Portuguese have appeared in anthologies such as *ACID+NEON* and *Contos de Tarot*. She was a first reader and editor of *A Taverna* magazine and is now a first reader of *Cascártica* magazine. In English, she has been published by *Skull & Laurel*. They are also a member of the Fantástico Guia, an organization that supports Brazilian speculative fiction writers who are writing and submitting their work in English.

CAROLINE SHEA is the author of *Lambflesh*. Her work has appeared in *Glass: A Journal of Poetry*, *Narrative Magazine*, and *Rogue Agent*, among other publications. You can be in touch and read more of her writing at caroline-fitzgerald-shea .squarespace.com.

STAFF BIOS

SEAN MARKEY publishes websites for a living and has always dreamed of publishing a magazine (about Death). He lives with his wife, Beth, in an old central Vermont farmhouse. Follow Sean on Twitter @PsychopompCom (if you want).

E. CATHERINE TOBLER is a writer and editor. You might know her editing work from *Shimmer Magazine*. You might know her writing from *Clarkesworld, Lightspeed,* and *Apex Magazine*. A trebuchet and Oxford comma enthusiast, she enjoys gelato and beer in her free time. Leo sun, Taurus moon. You can find her on Bluesky @ect.bsky.social.

NICASIO ANDRES REED is a writer, poet, and essayist whose work has appeared in venues such as *Shimmer, Fireside, Lightspeed,* and *Uncanny Magazine*. He's read slush for *Strange Horizons,* edited manuscripts for award-winning authors, and owns five different copies of *Moby Dick*. He lives with his family in Cavite province in the Philippines.

INKSHARK is a scandalously queer illustrator, author, and editor who lives in the rainy wilds of the Pacific Northwest. He enjoys exploring with his dogs, writing impossible things, and painting what he shouldn't. When his current meatshell begins to decay, he'd like science to put his brain into a giant killer octopus body with which he promises to be responsible and not even slightly shipwrecky. Pinky swear.

DAVID GILMORE is a writer, reader, and editor out of St. Louis, MO. His work has been featured in *The Rumpus* and at Lindenwood University, where he also received his MFA. He lives with his wife and son and spends his free time manning a stall in the Goblin Market selling directions to various Underworlds in exchange for rumors and information on where he can find his muse.

AMANDA DOWNUM is the author of *The Necromancer Chronicles, Dreams of Shreds & Tatters,* and the World Fantasy Award–nominated collection *Still So Strange.* Not content with armchair necromancy, she is also a licensed mortician. She lives in Austin, TX, with an invisible cat. You can summon her at a crossroads at midnight on the night of a new moon, or find her on Twitter as @stillsostrange.

LAURA BLACKWELL is a freelance copy editor and Shirley Jackson Award–winning writer. Her publications include stories in *Chiral Mad 5, Nightmare,* and the 2023 Shirley Jackson Award winner *Aseptic and Faintly Sadistic: An Anthology of Hysteria Fiction.* Visit her website—and if you like, sign up for her newsletter—at pronouncedlahra.com.

CHRISTINE M. SCOTT has been a professional graphic designer, website developer, and brand consultant for more than twenty-five years. She is the creative director and copublisher of Nosetouch Press and has coedited seven anthologies, including the folk horror anthology trilogy *The Fiends in the Furrows.* She is also an artist and craftsperson—several of her handcrafted items were included in *Game of Thrones: The Compendium,* printed by Chronicle Books for HBO. For a complete list of her pursuits, please visit christinemariescott.com.

FELICIA MARTÍNEZ is a writer and artist born and raised in Eastern New Mexico, though home is now the San Francisco Bay Area. She is a 2023 Dream Foundry Contest for Emerging Writers finalist, an honor she achieved with a beloved work of flash. Find her on Bluesky and Instagram as @feliciafm.

ANNIKA BARRANTI KLEIN is a freelance editor with a writing habit. Her work can be found at annikaobscura.com. She is supervised by a cat at all times.